The hint of a smile curved his lips

"What did you really expect to find when you ran away, Lanie? Was it this?"

His face was so close, she could practically taste him. But it wasn't her mouth his lips touched, it was the curve of her neck, a slow, hot, tasting caressing of his tongue. The fever blossomed, took away her breath, weakened her knees.

"Or this?"

His fingers slipped beneath the strap of her sundress, lowering it off her shoulder. His tongue traced a pattern from the curve of her collarbone to her shoulder and then to the swell of her breast.

Chris lifted his face and leaned very close to her so that his heat infused every pore, so close that his lips brushed hers when he spoke and she tasted, as well as heard, his words. "It's your fairy tale, Lanie Robinson. Tell me how it ends."

Dear Reader,

No doubt you've noticed the different look to your American Romance novels. Now you're about to discover what's new between the covers.

Come with us and sail the high seas with a swashbuckling modern-day pirate...ride off into the sunset on the back of a motorcycle with a dark and dangerous man...lasso a cowboy Casanova and brand him your own. You can do it all with the *new* American Romance!

In this book, and every book each month, you'll fall in love with our bold American heroes, the sexiest men in the world, as they take you on adventures that make their dreams—and yours—come true.

Enjoy the new American Romance—because love has never been so exciting!

Sincerely,

Debra Matteucci
Senior Editor & Editorial Coordinator
Harlequin Books
300 East 42nd St., 6th floor
New York, NY 10017

REBECCA FLANDERS

ONCE UPON A TIME

Harlequin Books

TORONTO • NEW YORK • LONDON
AMSTERDAM • PARIS • SYDNEY • HAMBURG
STOCKHOLM • ATHENS • TOKYO • MILAN
MADRID • WARSAW • BUDAPEST • AUCKLAND

Published September 1992

ISBN 0-373-16454-8

ONCE UPON A TIME

Chapter One

The last time Lanie Robinson ran away from home she had been eight years old. She had lost her shoe, fallen into a mud puddle and been chased by a dog. By the time darkness came she was more than happy to creep back home to supper with no one ever having been aware that she was gone.

Now, almost twenty-seven years later, Lanie Robinson's Great Escape II was turning out to be almost as inauspicious as her last one. The only difference between then and now was that this time home was almost twelve-hundred miles away. Her plane from Iowa had been late and she had missed her connection in Philadelphia. By the time she had finally arrived in Miami, the airport transportation had already departed, and she had had to find her own way to the port. Her luggage was lost. *She* was lost.

She paused to catch her breath, letting her heavy carry-on bag, oversized purse and bulky all-weather coat sink to the ground as she struggled to capture, even for a moment, that sense of heady triumph she was sure should be hers. After all, she had done it. Lanie Robinson—who had never traveled more than a hundred miles from home in her life—had scrawled a note, packed a bag and walked out on her home, job and family without a backward glance. She had made it this far; she wasn't about to turn back now.

She only wished she didn't have quite so far to go.

CHRISTOPHER VANDERMERE scrawled his signature on the last document just as the chauffeur-driven limousine pulled into the harbor area. He pushed up the tortoiseshell reading glasses and rubbed the bridge of his nose, scowling into the telephone. "Look, Madison, you can tell him for me—"

"If you don't mind, sir, I'd rather not." The crisp contralto tones of his secretary bore not the faintest hint of reproach—nor, in fact, any emotion at all. It was a pattern of speech that Elizabeth Madison, administrative assistant extraordinaire, had elevated to an art form. "If we might move on..."

Chris groaned out loud, letting the glasses drop painfully to the bridge of his nose again. "Move on?" He moved the telephone away from his face just long enough to tug the glasses off impatiently and toss them across the seat. Then he started to work on his tie. "I've got a stack of papers here tall enough to keep even you busy for the next month, two tapes of dictation are on the way to the office by special messenger as we speak, and if there's anyone in the continental United States I haven't talked to today it's only because I've faxed them. Please, don't you think I can go out and play now?"

He had been trying for five years to break through Madison's imperturbable facade and elicit a laugh, a chuckle, or even a small smile; mentally he marked down another failure as she replied, perfectly deadpan and without missing a beat, "In just one minute, sir. There are only a few more items we need to cover."

Chris was looking out the window, across the water, watching the harbor traffic with a quickening of his pulse and a deepening of anticipation that was so intense it was almost sexual. Only a few more minutes now and his escape would be complete. Meantime...

Chris got the tie off and tossed it the way of the glasses. His sigh was resigned as he shrugged out of his jacket and began working on the vest. "All right, go ahead."

THE MAN AT THE Great Escapes Tours booth had pointed Lanie in the direction of Pier Twenty-one and radioed the captain that she was on her way. He had neglected to mention that numbering the slips seemed to be irregular and optional. The last readable number had been Fifteen, and it felt to Lanie as though she had walked a mile since then. She had to be getting close.

She blotted her forehead with the cuff of her silk-blend blouse—which that morning had seemed so classy and stylish but was now as limp as her brand-new, guaranteed-not-to-frizz hairstyle—and shouldered her bags again with a muffled groan. She was wearing a skirt above her knees for the first time since puberty, and that made her self-conscious enough. But the pink wool was travel-creased and scratchy and completely inappropriate for Miami, even if it was January.

Two weeks sailing on a private yacht, maximum capacity six passengers, exploring small islands at which the bigger ships could never dock, scuba diving on coral reefs untouched by the tourist crowd, gourmet meals every night, being pampered from dawn to dusk…it was a dream come true. It didn't matter that Lanie did not know how to scuba dive, that she had never been sailing before in her life or that her idea of being pampered was Chinese takeout on Friday nights. It didn't even matter that this trip had taken every penny of her savings and most of her cash-advance limit on her credit card. This was her chance—quite possibly her last chance—to do something exciting, something unexpected, something purely because *she* wanted to do it. Nothing was going to stop her now...except, perhaps, missing the boat.

And then she saw Pier Twenty-one, and her spirits soared. The ship—boat, she corrected herself—was even more luxurious than the brochure had promised. Gleaming white and polished teak, it dwarfed its neighbors, both in size and beauty. The black letters across the side proclaimed its name to be *Serendipity* and Lanie broke into a rueful grin.

Not much about her life or even this trip had been serendipitous so far—but Lanie felt sure her luck was about to change.

VERY LITTLE OF Chris Vandermere's attention was on Elizabeth Madison's voice as he discarded his vest and pushed a button that lowered the tinted glass window. Almost immediately the climate-controlled interior of the limo was tainted by the smell of fish and salt and fuel, thick and humid and warm. Real air, real life. Chris inhaled deeply, unbuttoning the top three buttons of his shirt.

They passed Pier Eighteen, where the *Sunchaser,* a four-hundred-fifty-passenger cruiser, was docked; Pier Twenty, where the *Nordic Queen,* fifteen-hundred passengers, seventy-thousand tons, would be returning after a seven-day cruise to the Bahamas tomorrow at six a.m.; Pier Thirty, where the *Rendezvous,* the newest and some said the most luxurious cruise ship afloat was just now departing amid a rain of confetti and streamers for a two-week cruise of the Caribbean.

Chris did not have to glance out the window to identify the ships or even the piers they were passing. He knew them by smell, by feel, by the shadow they cast and the sound of their engines. The *Sunchaser,* the *Nordic Queen* and the *Rendezvous* were his, along with two other cruise ships docked in Miami and another three in Los Angeles. But they were business, and business was something he was in the process of shedding as systematically as he was his clothes. His mind was on the *Serendipity.*

"The board meeting has been confirmed for the fifteenth," Madison was saying. "That will give you two days after you return—"

"*If* I return."

That caused Madison to pause, and Chris experienced a small surge of satisfaction for having unsettled her, however temporarily. She recovered in less than a beat, however, and said, "If I may say, sir, that would be ill-advised at present...."

"I'm cutting this trip short as it is. What's the big deal if I miss one board meeting? There's nothing on the agenda that's not routine and Anthony has my proxy."

Again, a slight pause. Madison did not get along with Anthony and never had, which was one of the reasons Chris had put his brother in charge of west coast operations three years ago. The other reason, of course, was to simply give Anthony something to do.

"To be sure, sir, your brother is a fine young man, but with the situation being what it is I think your presence at the meeting would do a great deal to reassure the board members."

Chris scowled again. The last thing he wanted to think about now was the "situation" as it was. "The one thing that's guaranteed to *worry* the board members is my presence at a routine meeting," he pointed out, and not entirely facetiously. "Then they'll know something is wrong."

"Perhaps you're right, sir. Nonetheless—"

"Nonetheless," he interrupted firmly, "if I do decide to extend my trip you are *not* to send the coast guard looking for me. Is that clear?"

"Perfectly, sir." But Chris thought he detected a note of reluctance in her voice. "However, since you are occasionally out of radio contact—"

"I mean it, Madison."

"Yes, sir."

Score one for executive privilege, Chris thought grimly. But duty compelled him to say, "Is there anything else?" It didn't surprise him that there was.

THE GANGPLANK WAS one of those temporary, rolling structures that seemed to be attached to the boat more through good intentions than mechanical expertise, and Lanie clutched the handrail with both hands, lurching from side to side with each step. Her clattering approach must have been heard through the innermost reaches of the ship, for in only a moment the door to the cockpit opened and a man in yachting whites stepped on deck.

"Afternoon," he said, smiling.

He was middle-aged, fit and friendly-looking. "Hi," Lanie said, breathing hard. "Are you the captain?"

The smile widened into a grin as he touched the brim of his cap. "No, ma'am, afraid not. I guess you could call me the first mate, though. I'm Andrew, and Joel, here..." he nodded toward a younger man, also in white, who came around the side of the cockpit "...he'd be the crew. What can we do for you?"

"I'm Elaine Robinson. The captain is expecting me." She tried to shift around her carry-on bag and coat to get to her purse, where her boarding card was stored in one of the numerous compartments or pockets. "I'm sorry I'm late. I hope I haven't held you up too long."

There was only the slightest hesitance, and out of the corner of her eye Lanie saw the two men exchange a look. Then Andrew said, still in that warm, friendly voice, "No, you haven't held us up a bit. Mr. Vandermere isn't even here yet. Here, let me help you with that." He came forward to take her bag. "Joel, do you want to show the lady to the main cabin?"

Joel hurried forward with a quick "Welcome aboard, ma'am. Mind your step there."

He took her arm to help her on board, relieved her of the cumbersome coat and shouldered the bag Andrew passed to him. *Now this is more like it,* Lanie thought as he escorted her toward the main causeway.

Lanie had never been on anything bigger than a rowboat and she was fascinated by everything she saw. Unfortunately Joel moved too quickly for her to have much more than an impression of warm wood and polished brass, framed seascapes on the walls and rich carpeting underfoot.

"This is the main salon," Joel said when they went below deck. "Dinner is served here at eight, and you can find just about anything you want in the way of entertainment here. The galley is just beyond that hatch there, and the crew quarters and guest cabin are forward. Here you go."

He opened the door to another room and Lanie, feeling exactly like the wide-eyed tourist she was, dragged her attention to this new wonder with difficulty.

And it was a wonder. It was more of a suite than a cabin—a presidential suite at that. It was decorated in royal blue and gold with accents of rich wine, and every detail spoke of elegance and taste. The king-sized bed had massive posters, built-in cabinets underneath and an attached step stool for climbing into bed. Wall lamps cast romantic pools of light over the rich wood paneling, and silk draperies were drawn across a long high window. Two silk divans sidled up around an elegant Louis Quatorze card table laden with a basket of fruit, an enameled box of chocolates and a bottle of red wine.

"It's beautiful," Lanie breathed.

"You've never been on board the *Serendipity* before, ma'am?"

Lanie shook her head, her eyes straining to take in everything at once. "I've never even imagined anything like this."

Joel slid open the pocket door of a closet and set her bag inside, then hung up her coat. "She's some boat, all right. I think you'll find everything you need, ma'am," he said. "If not..." he indicated the telephone on the writing desk on one corner "...just pick up that phone and it rings the cockpit directly."

"Thank you," Lanie said, still a little dazzled as she looked around. "I can't think of a thing I could possibly need. Everything looks wonderful."

He smiled. "We're glad you could join us, after all. Mr. Vandermere called from his car about half an hour ago, so he should be arriving any minute now. As soon as he's on board we'll cast off."

"I'm glad I wasn't the only one who was late," Lanie said smiling.

He looked a little puzzled though his smile did not waver. "Yes, ma'am. Shall we notify you when he arrives?"

Lanie laughed. "Goodness, no. I imagine I'll notice when the boat starts moving. Will we be sailing into the sunset, do you think?"

The puzzlement in Joel's eyes became mixed with amusement as he paused at the door. "Actually," he explained, "we're on the east coast. Since the sun sets in the west..."

Lanie grinned, too exhilarated to be abashed. "No problem," she assured him. "It's just that I've always had this fantasy about sailing off into the sunset. Maybe next time, huh?"

Joe shared her grin. "Yes, ma'am. Be sure to call if you need anything."

When he was gone, Lanie flung her arms open wide, tossed back her head and whirled around the room, laughing in pure delight. Who would have thought that a trip that had begun so disastrously could end up like this?

When the Great Escapes brochure had described their adventure cruise on a private sailboat, Lanie had pictured something much more utilitarian. Naugahyde instead of silk... a compartment shower instead of a...

"Sunken tub," she breathed, peeking into the bathroom. And she clapped her hands together with another exclamation of laughter. It was almost too good to be true.

In Lanie's life there were traffic jams, overdue bills, school busses and alarm clocks. Missed connections and lost luggage were perfectly appropriate; sunsets, fairy tales and dreams come true were not. But this...

"I could definitely get used to this."

She stepped out of the scratchy pink skirt and stripped off her shoes and panty hose, letting them lie where they fell. Then, biting into one of the rich, imported chocolates, she climbed up on the big bed and propped two of the four pillows beneath her head. Two weeks of being pampered and catered to and living like a queen, with the creak of the timbers and the crack of the sails and the ocean stretching out around her in every direction, one long adventure waiting to be explored...

Oh, yes, she had made the right decision. She'd made her escape just in time.

CHRIS LIFTED HIS HIPS and tugged his shirttails out of his pants. "Did you ever hear anything from Hally?"

"Yes, sir. It seems he's visiting his daughter in California, but I'm assured by Peterson in personnel that the substitute crew is highly qualified."

Chris smothered a small oath. First the board meeting cutting into his getaway time, then one crisis after another delaying his departure, now Hally... Nothing about this trip was going right, and if he had been less stubborn, less brutally bent on his own pleasure, he would have gracefully accepted defeat and tried again for a better time. But defeat was something Christopher Vandermere had never had to learn to accept—gracefully or otherwise.

"Also, Miss Stephanie left word that she would call as soon as she's settled in her hotel in Amsterdam."

"That's one call I'll be glad to miss," Chris muttered.

"I imagine she's heard of ship to shore, sir."

"I wouldn't doubt you're right, Madison." Stephanie Orion, a fashion model with whom he had had a brief affair some years ago, had suddenly reappeared in his life several weeks back and invited herself along on this trip. Chris had hated the idea from the outset; he never brought women with him, had never even considered doing so, but somehow she had managed to rearrange all his plans and manipulate herself onto his guest list—along with half a dozen of her closest friends. That was until they had a huge fight and she stormed off to New York, and from there to Amsterdam. Looking back, Chris could see that Stephanie had been the bad omen that started all the trouble with this trip in the first place. Maybe there was something to that superstition about women and ships; he only knew he was glad to be rid of her.

They passed the busy pier area, and the car slowed as they approached the *Serendipity*'s dock. Chris felt his blood begin to thrum in response. "Wind it up, Madison." Cradling the telephone between his cheek and shoulder, he bent over to jerk his shoelaces loose. "I'm out of here in fifteen seconds."

"Have a good trip, sir," she responded, and disconnected.

Chris kicked off his shoes and pressed the intercom button that communicated with the front seat. "Dave, I've got a briefcase full of papers back here that needs to go back to the office, then you're free for the next two weeks. Have a good vacation."

"Thank you, Mr. Vandermere." The voice was tinny, but Dave made a circle of his thumb and forefinger and grinned at Chris in the rearview mirror. "You too."

"You'd better believe it."

Lastly, Chris stripped off his socks and tossed them into the pile with the other trappings of civilization. The man who stepped out of the limousine and bounded up the gangplank of the *Serendipity* was barefoot; the cuffs of his suit pants were rolled up above the ankles and his sleeves above the elbows. His open shirt billowed in the breeze as he swung on board, and he swept the two men who stood ready to greet him with a single glance.

"Chris Vandermere," he said, extending his hand to the older man.

"Andrew Keller. It's a pleasure, sir."

"Joel Webb. An honor to sail with you, sir."

Chris shook their hands, then looked them over frankly. "This is a two-man boat. I don't really need both of you."

Joel spoke up quickly. "I can sail, sir, but I signed on as steward and cook. That was back when your guest list was bigger, of course, but I was hoping for a chance to prove my usefulness anyway."

Chris hesitated for only a moment. "Well, I guess it won't kill us to eat something besides canned soup for two weeks. But the first time you light a candle or serve anything with a French name you walk the plank, understand? I get enough of that onshore."

Joel grinned. "Yes, sir. Meat and potatoes it is."

"Now you're catching on." Chris hoisted himself lightly to the low roof of the cockpit, checking the sails. "Gentlemen, we're going to get along just fine as long as you remember one thing. I'm the skipper. I'm not a passenger, not a guest, not the boss. We work together or not at all." He glanced at Andrew. "You want to tighten that line before we raise the mainsail."

"Yes, sir, right away."

"Drop the 'sir.' My name is Chris. And ditch the uniforms, will you? This isn't the navy."

Andrew grinned, and both men relaxed visibly. "First chance I get. By the way, the young lady is settled comfortably, so we can cast off whenever you're ready."

"Good for her," Chris muttered absently. "Although why she thinks I should care..." He checked the jib and the winch, and satisfied, turned back to Andrew. "All right, throttle her up. Let's see if we can get out of the harbor before dark."

He sprang back down to the deck, and then he noticed Joel staring at his feet. He grinned. "For a real sailor, bare feet are safer on deck than any shoe you can buy. I learned that from my grandfather, who learned it from his grandfather, and *he*" Chris winked "—was a pirate."

Joel smiled at him uncertainly. "Yes, sir—I mean, Chris. I'll have to try that."

Chris laughed and made his way toward the bow. He was at home, he was free, and even the company of strangers was exhilarating. "Get the stern, will you, Joel? Let's blow this town."

Chris raised his voice to be heard by Andrew in the cockpit. "Cast off!"

He caught the bowline and released it with a snap; Joel did the same with the stern. The pilot engine powered up and the boat began to inch away from the dock. His feet planted firmly as he coiled the line, Chris threw back his head and drew the tangy salty air deep into his lungs. When the boat cleared the dock he felt something inside him break free, as though the invisible line that tied him to the world onshore had snapped.

Responsibility, schedules, commitments, decisions—they all began to sink into the great melting pot called civilization, and no longer had anything do with Chris Vandermere. Before him the harbor stretched like a gateway to forever, beyond it the open sea. For the next two weeks he was as free as any man who ever lived: a man and the sea, testing each other and proving each other as they had done since the beginning of time.

Nothing was going to spoil his pleasure now.

LANIE AWOKE with a start... and an overwhelming sense of disorientation. But the sight of the luxurious room and the sounds that had awakened her—the creak of boards, the snap of the sails, the muffled sounds of footsteps and voices overhead—reminded her where she was.

She smiled drowsily and leaned back onto the pillows. God, she was hungry. Back home, if she didn't have dinner on the table for her niece and nephew by five-thirty, her sister, Cassie, would launch into her nutrition speech.

Lanie wondered what they were all doing for dinner tonight, and she even tried to muster up a thread of wistfulness for the family she had left behind. But she found, much to her delight, that she could barely remember their faces.

"I hope they starve," she murmured out loud, and a deliciously wicked grin spread across her face. Freedom. It was a heady thing.

She got to her knees and pushed back a corner of the heavy drape that obscured the window over the bed. She could see nothing but a dusky blue sea and the faintest glimpse of a paler gray horizon in the distance. Wonder washed over her at the sight. She had done it. She was at sea, all by herself on a sailing vessel bound for exotic locales. She could see the ocean and the spray against the window, she could feel the motion of the waves, but she still could hardly believe it was real. She half expected to wake up at any moment and find herself dozing in a crowded airport somewhere between Florida and Iowa, or worse, back in her own bed at home.

She heard the door open behind her and that was when she knew she wasn't asleep at all. She whirled instinctively, gasping as she scrambled to pull the coverlet up over her legs. She assumed that it must have been Joel, and she must not have heard him knock.

But it wasn't Joel. And the man who stood there made no move to depart.

Maybe it was the surprise, or the way he stood there on the threshold, boldly regarding her as she tried frantically to cover her naked thighs. Something had stripped Lanie of speech and left her, for a moment, incapable of doing anything but stare back at him.

He might have been in his mid-thirties, with thick chestnut hair that was dappled with sea dew, and very, very green eyes. He was wearing a white dress shirt, open over a smooth golden chest and sleeves folded back to his elbows. His feet were bare, the cuffs of his pants wet despite the fact that they were rolled up to his calves. He was of average height or a little taller with the long-lined muscles of a tennis player or a runner, or perhaps a weekend sailor. Lanie's eyes kept returning to his torso. There was something about that shirt—water-splotched and unbuttoned, exposing his tanned chest and forearms—that struck Lanie as the sexiest thing she had ever seen.

She jerked her eyes away from his torso and managed, with as much dignity as she could possibly muster, "Excuse me?"

His eyes moved over her once more, quite coolly it seemed to Lanie, and he replied, "Not very likely."

He stepped inside and closed the door.

Oddly enough, the first thing Chris had noticed when he opened the door was the pair of black pumps

discarded carelessly on the floor. It took him several
seconds to follow the trail of panty hose and skirt toward the figure on the bed, and by then he was not in
a good mood at all.

The woman wasn't exactly what he might have expected to find, which was to say she was neither
young, blond, voluptuous or naked. Not that she
didn't, of course, have a certain unique appeal all her
own. With brown hair shag-cut and rumpled, and
nondescript brown eyes, she was just enough of a departure from the stereotypical sex kitten to be intrigu-
ing, and Chris found that a little disturbing.

Yet he kept his manner casual as he strode into the
room. "There are several possible explanations for
this," he said easily, "and I've got to warn you I can't
find one of them I like. This is just the sort of trick old
Hally would like to play, but frankly I don't think he'd
go to the trouble to arrange it all the way from California."

He bent and picked up the panty hose, held it up for
a moment with his thumb and forefinger, then carefully arranged it over the back of a chair. She watched
him with big doe eyes.

"My secretary, who *could* have arranged it, has absolutely no sense of humor, so that lets her off the
hook. We're down to two possibilities."

He picked up the pink wool skirt, shook out the
wrinkles, and held it up for a moment, too, measur-

ing the length. From what he had been able to see before she'd swaddled her lower body in his comforter, she had very nice legs, and it looked as though the skirt were designed to show them to advantage.

He folded the skirt on the chair next to the panty hose. "If you belong to Joel or Andrew," he said, "I'd like to think they'd have better sense than to put you in my cabin. So." At last he bent down and picked up the shoes, arranging them neatly side by side on the chair seat. "Do you by any chance know a woman named Stephanie?"

She was pressed as far back against the headboard as she could go. The expression in her eyes was no longer just wary; she looked at him the way one might a mad dog who could spring at any moment. "Who *are* you?" she gasped hoarsely.

Chris smiled thinly, invoking a lazy, pleasured malice as his eyes moved over her. "I, my dear, am not a nice guy." He came toward her with a smooth, measured stride, keeping his voice low and deliberate. With every step he took she shrank back farther against the headboard. "I am what is known as a corporate giant, a captain of industry, a maker of kings. The earth shakes when I walk. Governments quake when I frown, nations cower when I roar."

He stood over her now, and her eyes were huge as she looked up at him, still shrinking back. He braced his hands on the headboard and leaned down low over her, and she couldn't shrink back any farther. "So roll your video camera," he said softly, "set up your stills, and make a copy for me, will you? There's nothing you can do that will even embarrass me, much less interest me enough for blackmail, because I can just about promise you that not only have I already done it, I've probably already got it on film."

Chapter Two

Lanie's pulse was pounding dryly in her throat. She knew she should scream for help, lunge for the telephone, put into practice what she could recall of that two-day self-defense course she had taken at the Y, or at least *threaten* to do so. But he was so close she could smell the sea on his skin, and she couldn't see anything but his eyes. And all she could manage was, "Who are you? What are you doing here?"

Something close to puzzlement crept into his eyes, and a hint of amusement softened his mouth. After a moment he straightened up, and answered in a somewhat more relaxed tone of voice, "I'm Christopher Vandermere. I own this boat. This is my cabin. You are in my bed. Now, may I ask you the same questions?"

Lanie jerked her chin up and clutched at bravado as desperately as she held on to the sheet that was wound around her hips. "You most certainly may not! You come barging into a woman's room—"

"Cabin."

"Without even knocking, making all sorts of weird demands..." The courage she had feigned was gradually becoming real, fueled by genuine indignation. "If you don't leave here this minute I'm going to call security—"

"If you don't give me some answers this minute I'm going to throw you overboard."

His tone was flat and matter-of-fact and the way he said that—the way he looked at her—in fact, everything about him, left very little doubt in Lanie's mind that he meant it. He just stood there with his arms crossed on his chest, watching her with that spark of cautious, speculative amusement in his eyes. In the dimly lit room, with his bare feet and open shirt and wind-tossed hair, he reminded Lanie of a pirate, toying with his victim before he made a final decision as to her fate.

Lanie swallowed dryly, holding on to her courage—and her composure—with a definite effort now. "I'm Lanie Robinson," she replied coolly, "and there's obviously been some mix-up about the rooms. I have my boarding card in my purse."

"Your what?"

"My boarding card. If you'll just give me a minute—"

"Let me understand this." For a moment he looked almost as confused as she was. "You're not a leftover from Stephanie's party? She didn't send you?"

"I don't know any Stephanie. I booked this trip through a travel agent in Cedar Rapids, Iowa—"

"*Where?*"

"And if you'll just give me a minute to get dressed we can go see the captain and—"

"I *am* the captain."

The amusement in his eyes had been replaced with a scowl as dark as night water, and as he stood there glaring down at her he seemed to grow more formidable. Yes, he probably was the captain *and* the owner of this yacht, and it probably was his cabin and his bed. That was the kind of day she was having... the kind of *life* she was having.

She cleared her throat, met his eyes, and with as much dignity as possible said, "Would you hand me my skirt, please?"

He just looked at her.

On the other hand, she hadn't exactly picked this cabin out by multiple choice. It wasn't *her* fault the steward had made a mistake. She had paid good money for this cruise and he had no right to treat her like a criminal, no matter who he was.

Her back teeth ground together in the way they had of doing when she was trying not to be annoyed, and she said coolly, "Since you obviously aren't going to be a gentleman and wait outside, the least you can do is let me stand up.''

After a moment he scooped up her skirt and tossed it to her. ''A gentleman is something I have to be when I go to the opera, not when I'm in international waters on my own boat.''

''Turn around.''

''What?''

''Turn your head so I can get dressed.''

The spark of amusement crept back into his eyes. Lanie was not sure that she liked that wicked little smile that curved his lip any more than his scowl.

''Your modesty's a little late, don't you think? After all, I saw most of what you have to offer when I came in.''

She did not dignify that with a reply, but held his eyes defiantly.

The unpleasant glint in his eyes faded, but the smile lingered. ''You're serious, aren't you?''

She waited. Eventually he turned his back on her.

Lanie carefully unwound the coverlet from around her hips, watching him all the while. She crawled to the edge of the bed.

''Iowa, did you say?''

She kept her eyes on him, but he did not turn around. ''That's right.''

''That would explain the shoes.''

She stepped into the skirt and pulled it up quickly over her hips. "What?"

"Nothing."

He turned around, smiling, just as Lanie was tugging the back zipper of her skirt closed. She scowled at him irritably, trying to stuff her blouse back into the waistband. "I didn't say you could turn around. How did you know I was ready?"

"The sound of a zipper in the dark. There's nothing quite like it." Then he gestured toward the mirror on the wall he had been facing, through which he had been able to observe her every movement. "Not much of a trick, really."

Angry and embarrassed, color suffused her cheeks, and she did her best to ignore it—and him—as she stalked toward the writing desk where she had dropped her purse. "My cabin assignment is on my boarding card. It'll just take a minute to find out where I'm supposed to be."

She jerked open the drawstring of her purse and dipped her hand inside, coming up with her wallet, a hairbrush, a package of tissues and a book of matches. She slapped them on the desk. "Although if you want to know the truth, I'm not very impressed with the way you run your ship—or with your manners, when it comes to that."

A bottle of aspirin, a sewing kit, umbrella and bag of peanuts she had gotten on the plane joined the pile on the table. Chris took a curious step forward.

"It was your steward who made the mistake, you know—if, of course, you are who you say you are. I'm going to want some proof of that before I give up this cabin, by the way."

Chris watched in growing amazement as a corkscrew, a folded plastic poncho and a small tool kit were added to the collection on the desk. He said, "I'm waiting for you to pull a small sports car out of there. Then I'll leave."

She shot him a dark glance. "I also have mace. But they wouldn't let me bring it on the plane."

"Wise decision."

"There!" she exclaimed triumphantly, and held up the boarding card. "It says here, dock Twenty-one." She turned the bright pink card over. "Cabin C. What cabin is this?"

Chris said, "May I see that?"

She handed the card to him. He examined it for a moment, then glanced up at her. "Great Escapes Tours?"

Something about the way he said that caused a thread of uneasiness to snake through Lanie. She nodded.

Chris picked up the telephone.

"Andrew," he said, "there's a young lady in my cabin who says my steward brought her here. Would you like to tell me what you know about it?" A pause while he listened. Then, "I see." A question. He answered, "As a matter of fact I don't." Another pause, then, "Yes, I'm sure you are. But that doesn't help much now, does it? What's our position?"

The pause seemed longer this time, and not all of it was spent listening to the other man's reply. Then he swore, tersely and succinctly, and said, "No, hold the course. I'll let you know."

He replaced the receiver and turned back to Lanie. There was no humor in his eyes at all now, and the line of his mouth was grim. "I don't know how you did it," he said, and returned the boarding card to her with a snap, "but you're on the wrong boat."

The strength left Lanie's knees and she didn't fight it. She sank into the nearest chair. She looked up at him and all she could think to say was, "I guess that means you didn't find my luggage."

Chris plunged his hands into the pockets of his trousers, glaring at her in a way that might indeed have made governments quake, but Lanie was too stunned to notice. "Well, Miss Lanie Robinson from Cedar Rapids, Iowa—"

"Camden," she corrected automatically. "Camden is where I'm from, Cedar Rapids is just the nearest big town. And you don't really care, do you?"

"That's right, I don't. You're in a hell of a mess, do you know that?"

She said glumly, "I've spent every penny I have for a two-week nonrefundable cruise and I missed the boat. I'm a stowaway on a private yacht in the middle of the ocean with three men I've never met before. No one knows where I am. I don't even have any luggage. Yeah, I'd say this is what you could call a hell of a mess."

Chris's frown deepened. "I suppose you expect me to take you back to Miami."

She lifted her shoulders dispiritedly. "What for? The boat I'm supposed to be on is long gone."

Chris swore again and turned away from her, thrusting his fingers through his hair in a single angry gesture. She was on his boat where she had no business being, interfering with his plans, ruining what might well be his last chance to get away this winter, and the last thing he wanted to do was feel sorry for her.

He had to take her back, he knew that. Of course, if they returned to the harbor now they wouldn't be able to set sail again until morning. It wasn't just the wasted hours that went against the grain with Chris, it was the principle. Once he had set course, any course, he wasn't accustomed to turning back.

But any way he looked at it, his vacation was ruined.

He turned back to her with terse words on his lips but she looked so dejected sitting there that the words died unspoken. "Look," he said on a calming breath. "It's been a long day and I need a shower and a drink."

"I know the feeling."

Chris hesitated only a minute, then said shortly, "Oh, all right. You can use the bath in here and we'll meet for a drink in the main salon. Maybe I'll figure out what to do by then." He opened one of the storage drawers under the bed and withdrew several items of clothing. "Don't use all the hot water," was all he said as he left. After his appalling behavior, it galled Lanie to do as he said. But, she realized quickly, she was rather dependent upon him for a few small things—like food, water and transportation home.

She doubted a mere shower would make her feel better. And she was right.

Thanks to her credo, Everything that can go wrong will go wrong, her carry-on bag was almost as well stocked as her purse. She pulled out a sundress. It would have to make do for having drinks with a man who looked capable of setting her adrift without food or water. She ran a brush through her hair—it still felt odd to reach up and find several inches of it missing—and even applied a thin coat of lipstick. Then she carefully repacked her belongings, straightened the rumpled bed and shouldered both bags. With one last look around the cabin to make sure everything was exactly as she had found it, she left the room.

Chris was waiting for her in the main salon. Despite the preoccupied frown on his face, he looked much less formidable now in faded jeans and a long-sleeved, equally faded cotton shirt. He was lounging back on one of the wide sofas, one bare foot propped up on its surface, a glass of a pale amber liquid in his hand. He looked up when Lanie came out, and swung his foot to the floor.

"I would have fixed you a drink," he said, gesturing toward the open bar, "but I didn't know what you liked."

Lanie let her bags slide to the floor outside the cabin door. "Something strong," she said. "Like hemlock."

He grinned and got to his feet. "Out of stock. How about whiskey?"

"Sure."

He dropped ice into a short glass, poured a splash of whiskey over it, then, glancing at her, added a liberal dose of water.

"Right," she said, smiling wryly. "I don't drink much."

He raised his glass to her. "This seems like as good a time as any to start."

She returned his salute. "I'll drink to that." And she did.

He gestured her to be seated and she chose one of the sofas. Chris pulled out a club chair and sat opposite her. A succulent aroma emanated from the kitchen and Lanie's stomach growled. She hoped he would at least feed her before he threw her overboard.

Chris said abruptly, "The situation is this. I don't like to return to harbor at night. We're out of the traffic lanes now and at a safe anchor point. We'd be a lot better off to stay where we are and head back in the morning."

Lanie smiled without enthusiasm. "You're the captain." Then, with slightly more conviction, "I'm really sorry for the inconvenience."

He sipped from his glass. "It can't be helped now. Listen, Joel radioed that tour company of yours. They said they're sorry but there's not much they can do for you. You could probably get them to apply a partial credit to another tour, if you're willing to hang around for another ten days until the next boat leaves."

Lanie drew a deep breath and released it slowly, giving a philosophical shake of her head. "No, I guess not. Obviously I wasn't meant for an adventure tour. I'm just not the type."

"I don't know," Chris observed. "It looks to me like you're having a pretty big adventure now."

Lanie laughed softly. "I guess I am." The smile they shared lingered, and Lanie began to relax.

It occurred to Lanie that the last thing she should be feeling in this situation was relaxed.

Back in the cabin he had looked intimidating—there was no point in denying that. But now he looked... comfortable. Comfortable, at ease, and subtly, inarguably sexy.

A good half of his shirt was carelessly undone and the pale red, oft-washed material seemed to caress the shape of his torso. His jeans were battered and frayed at the knees and hem, worn almost white where jeans would receive the most wear—at the knees, across the fly, on the inside of the thighs. These were working jeans, well-worn and loved, not too tight but well fitting enough to show off the essentials to advantage. And though she had never before imagined there could be anything sexy about a man's bare feet there was something about strong masculine ankles that seemed to her incredibly suggestive.

Lanie was around men every day, most of them young, strong and—in their own opinions, at least—walking examples of sexuality perfected. Perhaps she had grown immune to the various elements of obvious appeal, or perhaps there was something in the sea air that had awakened long-dormant sensitivities. Because it had been a long, long time since she had admired a man simply for the pleasure of it.

But when she caught her eyes traveling back to the faded denim across his fly she stopped herself and took another quick sip of her drink. There was no place to look then except at his face, and the lazy speculative smile that curved his lips and played in his eyes brought a quick unwelcome heat to her cheeks.

She dropped her eyes to her glass and then looked back at him. Her throat felt a little tight, her heart pounded out a few uncomfortable beats. She blurted, "If I asked you to—would you take me back tonight?"

That half-amused, far-too-knowledgeable smile only deepened, and he tipped his glass toward her in an idle salute. "Not a nice guy, remember?"

Lanie stiffened her shoulders. "Listen, I think there's something we should get straight."

But she had lost his attention. His eyes moved over her shoulder as the swinging door behind her opened and annoyance replaced the suggestive gleam. "For God's sake, Joel, I told you no candles. And what is that, a tablecloth?"

Joel hesitated before the table, a white damask cloth folded over one arm and two candlesticks in the other hand. "I'm sorry, sir. I thought since the lady was dining, too..."

Chris waved a dismissing hand. "Just bring the food."

"Yes, sir."

When he was gone, Lanie said wryly, "I was going to tell you not to waste any energy trying to seduce me—"

"Let me assure you. Tablecloths and candlesticks are not among my tools of seduction."

Lanie thought it best not to encourage that line of conversation. The chandelier swayed very gently with the soft rise and fall of the ocean that surrounded them, and the muffled creak of the timbers was soothing. Lanie was beginning to feel the effects of the whiskey, warm and relaxing.

"It's probably rude of me to ask," she said, "but I don't get to meet too many corporate giants. Exactly what kind of industry are you a captain of?"

"Shipping," he replied. "I'm CEO and chief shareholder in the Holland-Alaska cruise line."

"Holland-Alaska? That seems like an unlikely combination to me."

He shrugged. "It's a long story, entwined with family history, and doesn't have anything to do with the ships' registries."

"Holland-Alaska," Lanie mused, her brow puckering with thought. "I looked at a lot of cruise brochures. Would I know any of your ships?"

Joel returned with a large serving tray and began setting out dinner. Chris got to his feet, gesturing her to precede him. "Have you ever heard of the *Rendezvous?*"

"Do you mean that ship with the enclosed aviarium and the three-story chandelier? And the crystal piano in the rotating lounge?"

"That's the one."

"My goodness." She stared at him in unabashed admiration as she stood up. "You *are* richer than God."

"I know a few shareholders who'd argue with you there," he replied ruefully. "Until the *Rendezvous* starts turning a profit, we're lucky to make payroll. Careful, there."

An unexpected sway of the boat caused Lanie to lose her balance and lurch into him. He caught her arm, steadying her with a firm grip. The flesh of her upper arm was smooth and soft beneath his fingers, the curve of her breast brushed against his chest. She smelled of the citrus-scented soap with which the decorator had stocked his showers, and nothing else. Her face, upturned and looking a little breathless, was faintly flushed—perhaps with the effects of the alcohol, or perhaps in response to his touch. It occurred to Chris, and not for the first time, that there were certain advantages to having an unexpected guest on board—particularly when that guest was female and as attractive as this Lanie Robinson.

"Haven't gotten your sea legs yet, eh?" He chuckled softly, releasing her arm but keeping his fingertips lightly on her bare back as he escorted her to the table.

"Guess not," she agreed as he pulled out the chair for her.

Lanie liked the way his eyes crinkled and sparkled when he laughed, like a man looking into the sun. In his faded shirt with his laughing eyes he did not look like the chief shareholder in a major cruise line, or the CEO of anything. He looked like someone Lanie could be comfortable with, and easily grow to like.

Joel poured two glasses of red wine, and Lanie unfolded her napkin in her lap. Chris eyed the artfully arranged salad that was set before him on a crystal plate and said, "Where did you get the fancy dishes? I don't remember having anything like this on board."

"Apparently they're leftover from the party, sir. I found a box marked with the name of a catering company. I wouldn't have opened it but I didn't find any salad plates in your regular stock."

Chris muttered, "You wouldn't." He picked up his salad fork. "What's the main course?"

"Boeuf bourg—that is, beef stew, sir. Chris."

Chris shot him an amused look. "You're learning. And it smells good, even if it does have a French name."

Joel seemed encouraged by his approval, and he turned to Lanie. "Miss Robinson," he said earnestly, "on behalf of Andrew and myself I'd like to apologize for the mix-up. I hope everything can be worked out for you, and if there's anything I can do just ask."

"Don't be silly, it wasn't your fault. But if you'd really like to do something for me . . ."

He looked at her inquiringly.

"Something really fattening for dessert would go a long way toward cheering me up."

Joel smiled. "Leave it to me. I've got a Death by Chocolate that's illegal in several countries."

Lanie laughed, and when he was gone she turned back to Chris, picking up her salad fork. "I hope you don't blame your crew," she said seriously. "They had no way of knowing I didn't belong on board."

Chris looked annoyed. "Maybe. But it seems to me they could have been a little more careful and saved us all a lot of trouble." Lanie tried not to let the comment sting.

"Anyway," he went on, "they're not my crew, they're just hired help. I usually sail with Hally—he's an old sea dog who takes care of some of the boats at the marina, the *Serendipity* included. But he's in California somewhere so someone from the office pulled these guys from the personnel pool. What do you want to bet Joel's auditioning for a chef's job on one of the big ships?"

"He's got my vote," she replied. "What's this about a party? Am I a gate-crasher on top of everything else?"

He winced. "Believe me, no. Another long, ugly story. But it might explain some of the confusion that made it easier for you to get on board. An old friend of mine—or should I say an ex-friend of mine—thought she'd take advantage of my good nature by inviting a bunch of people along for the cruise. I managed to cancel it just in time."

Lanie lifted her wine glass. "Or almost in time, anyway."

Chris grinned. "Right."

He was enjoying the evening much more than he had expected to, and than he had intended to, under the circumstances. He didn't like to have his plans thrown into disarray and he couldn't say he was glad that this strange woman had decided to stow away on his boat. He had to admit it wasn't half-bad.

He had to admire her poise. From the way she had discreetly inquired about his finances to the way she had put Joel at his ease, she had demonstrated a friendly forthright manner that Chris doubted he could have maintained under the circumstances. And if the truth be told she wasn't terribly hard to look at across a dinner table. The bright striped sundress hugged breasts that were high and round and nicely full, defining them in a way that kept drawing Chris's eyes back to the row of white anchor-shaped buttons that closed the garment down the front. The dress was tight across the torso and abdomen but the skirt was full, gracing her calves in a very attractive way. She had brushed her hair in nice smooth lines that tempted him to tousle it with his hands and the salon's soft highlighting gave her face a delicate glow.

"You know," he said as Joel took away the salad plates, "you're really taking this quite well. Most women would be hysterical by now."

She toyed with her fork. "That wouldn't help matters, would it?" And she gave a light lift of her shoulders. "Besides, I'm kind of used to things like this. Not," she assured him with a smile, "that I get on the wrong boat every day of my life. Let's just say I'm no stranger to disappointment. That looks great," she told Joel as he placed a plate of boeuf bourgignon before her.

Chris knew there was a story behind her words, perhaps several, and he determined not to pursue it. He would have dinner with her, he'd enjoy looking at her, he'd even have a conversation with her, but he refused to get involved with this woman. That was not what he had come out here for.

"I don't have anything to do with assigning chefs," he told Joel as he was served. "You should see Hawkins in Personnel."

Joel looked surprised, but murmured only, "Thank you, I will. Enjoy your dinner."

Lanie picked up her fork. "You know, I was afraid I'd get seasick, but so far I feel great." Then she looked up at him, a startled look of amused chagrin on her face. "Oops. That wasn't a very good conversational gambit for the dinner table, was it?"

Chris chuckled. She *was* fun. "Actually, we're in pretty calm waters, so I'd be surprised if you did get sick. But this boat is fairly stable and big enough that you shouldn't have a problem unless we hit some rough seas."

"How big is it?"

"Forty foot."

"Well, no wonder I made the mistake. The boat I was supposed to be on was only thirty-six feet. Obviously I have a taste for luxury, even if I don't have very good eyesight." She tasted the beef. "This is marvelous. Tell me about the *Rendezvous*. That must have been quite an undertaking."

"It was," Chris agreed. "Of course it was really my father's project. If it had been up to me I would have started from scratch but we purchased the ship to refurbish during my father's time so I had to follow through."

"But I thought the *Rendezvous* was a new ship."

"It is—to us. That's the way it is in the cruise business. Very few new ships are built. Most of the ones that are introduced as new are just middle-aged gals with a face-lift transferred from one line to another, spruced up, renamed. Of course the *Rendezvous* was redesigned from stem to stern...."

And there he was, before he knew it, talking about his work, which was exactly what he had sought to escape, and making dinnertime conversation, which he hated. It wasn't just any conversation but conversation about the *Rendezvous,* his folly, the one thing he had promised himself he would *not* think about while he was away. How did she do it? How had he allowed himself to be manipulated into this?

But she kept asking questions, the way a woman well trained in conversation does without even trying, and he kept answering because... because he wanted to. And that was the trouble. He was enjoying her company far too much. Simply being with her was lulling him back into all the habits and thought patterns he had thought he'd left behind the moment he set foot on the *Serendipity.*

By the time Joel came to take away the plates Chris could feel the restlessness crawling on his skin, and he knew he had a choice: he could stay here the rest of the evening and watch the way the swaying of the chandelier caught the highlights in Lanie's hair or he could go up on deck, where the captain of a vessel belonged. He was surprised and a little dismayed at how long it took him to make that decision.

Abruptly he stood, tossing his napkin on the table. "It's my turn for watch. Good night."

And without another word or backward glance, he left.

Chapter Three

She spotted his silhouette at the rail. He stood motionless, awash in moon glow.

The anchor lights, high in the mast and around the outer hull, provided the only illumination, but it was enough for Lanie to make her way carefully around the rail. The sea was a deep rich indigo occasionally frothed with white, and the clouds, like tufts of floating cotton, were surreally backlit. The deck beneath her stockinged feet was damp with spray, rising and falling in slow, rocking sighs that were only slightly out of sync with the creaking of the mast. A warm breeze tickled her skin and ruffled her hair, and as far as she could see there was nothing but still, dark night. It was almost breath-robbingly beautiful, serene and poignant at the same time, and even when Lanie reached the forward deck she didn't speak right away, but stood beside Chris at the rail, inhaling the sea-thick air and letting the moment imprint itself on her memory.

There was a distant splash and Chris lifted his arm, pointing ahead. "There," he said softly. "Did you see it? A porpoise. There's a whole school of them out there. I've been watching them for a while."

Lanie shook her head, straining in the darkness toward the direction he pointed. "No, I can't see anything."

"It'll take a few minutes for your night vision to kick in."

He was leaning forward, resting his forearms on the rail, and when he turned his head to look at her Lanie was struck by what a powerful figure he made with the night wind in his hair and the sea in his eyes. Muscles relaxed, face half-shadowed in quiet contemplation, completely at ease against this vast backdrop of ocean and sky, he looked like a man who was exactly where he belonged.

Lanie was reminded then of why she had come on deck. "Listen, I don't mean to bother you. I know I'm probably not allowed up here. I just wondered where you wanted me to sleep tonight."

Chris looked her over thoroughly and with leisure. The sea breeze ruffled her hair, leaving it soft and tousled in that bedroom way Chris had first admired. The flared skirt of her dress alternately billowed and shaped her body from pelvis to knee; it was easy to imagine his hands doing the same thing. Easy to imagine his hands nestling over the soft full flesh of

her breasts in the same way the material of her dress
was doing now; so easy in fact that he felt a very real
tightening of his loins in response to the picture in his
mind. Easy to imagine the taste of her on his tongue,
the hot wet inner recesses of her mouth, the tangy cit-
rus taste of her skin, the musky silk of her most secret
places . . .

Where did he want her to sleep tonight? The answer to that was far, far too easy; its inevitability a
prospect he preferred to savor.

So he turned back to his view of the sea and replied, "What do you mean, you're not allowed up
here? I'm not Captain Bly, you know."

"I thought you wanted to be alone."

A rueful smile touched his lips. "I guess I was a little rude earlier."

"You missed a great dessert."

"But you missed the porpoises."

Lanie could have pointed out that she hadn't been
invited to view the porpoises. But his smile was too
warm, his eyes too entrancing. All she could do was
smile back.

He glanced at her. "Look, I'm sorry. It's nothing
personal, really, it's just that I have a pretty fixed idea
about how these voyages are supposed to be, and to
tell the truth nothing has gone the way I planned since
I set out."

Lanie could not prevent a rueful smile of her own. "I know how that is."

"Yeah, I guess you do."

"What was it supposed to be like?" she asked. "Since you canceled the party, that is."

A private amusement crept into his tone. "Well, there weren't supposed to be any women aboard for one thing. It's just a chance for me to get away for a while, to get sweaty and let my beard grow and get drunk late at night and tell dirty jokes..."

"Man things," supplied Lanie sagely.

"Right. Life the way it was meant to be lived. Also, this is the only place in the known universe where I can't be reached by phone. You wouldn't believe what a load just knowing that takes off my mind."

"Don't you have a radio?"

"Ah, but the beauty of a radio is that if you don't want to talk, you turn it off."

Lanie shook her head, a little overwhelmed by the effort it took to even imagine the kind of life he led. "And then I come along and remind you of everything you're trying to get away from, asking a thousand questions, making you talk about your work."

He looked a little surprised at how quickly she understood, then he looked back over the rail. "It's not the end of the world. Worse things have happened to me, believe me. Worse things have happened to you today alone."

That made her laugh. "Okay, we won't argue about who's had the worst day. I have a feeling we're not even in the same arena."

Chris smiled to himself in the dark, all alone where she couldn't see, and his amusement held a touch of resignation. He had come on deck to get away from her and the responsibilities and echoes of the onshore world she represented, but he had spent most of his time thinking about her. Women like Lanie Robinson didn't blunder into his life every day; opportunities like the one she represented were too rare to be missed.

Why fight it? he thought. It was only for one night.

He said, "Look. Right where I'm pointing."

Lanie tried to follow the direction of his arm, but although she could hear the splash of porpoises at play she could see nothing.

Chris stepped away from the rail and moved behind her, gently framing her head with his hands and guiding it to the left, lining up her vision with his. For a moment she was so startled by the sensation of the warm body next to hers, his strong, slender fingers on her hair, that she couldn't concentrate on anything except the surprised, leaping tumble of her heart within her chest. And then she saw a flash of movement in the distance, a cascade of water shimmering in reflected light. She caught her breath and then she spotted it—the graceful arc of a porpoise by starlight, slicing through the air in a graceful, joyous dance before returning, once again, to the sea.

"Oh . . . my," Lanie breathed.

Chris let his hands linger just a moment longer against the clean, silky texture of her hair, his face close to hers as he shared her vision of the sea. The sweet lemony fragrance that clung to her skin reminded him of lazy summer afternoons and seemed to blend into the warm night air as though it were born there. He enjoyed the awe he felt from her as she discovered for herself one of the sea's simple wonders, for no matter how often he made such discoveries for himself there was nothing quite like the first time.

He held her for a deliberate second, or perhaps two, too long—until he could feel the change in her, a subtle tensing of her muscles, a shift in her level of awareness. He savored her response, let it linger in the air between them for another two heartbeats, and then he stepped casually away.

Lanie drew in a deep breath, as much to calm the sudden fluttery state of her nerves as for the rich aroma of sea air that she craved. "This is incredible, isn't it? Now I understand why people go sailing."

Chris didn't return to his position at the rail but stood close beside her, enjoying her nearness and indulging himself in the simple pleasure of *her* pleasure. He said, "This isn't sailing. Sailing is mostly about being cold and wet and sticky with salt, about clogged plumbing and moldy bread and putting on damp underwear every morning.''

"If this isn't sailing, what is it?"

"Yachting."

"What's the difference?"

"Yachting is a gentleman's sport. Sailing is a way of life."

Lanie was thoughtful for a moment. "I know I probably should think the opposite, with your being a corporate giant and all, but you strike me as more of a sailor than a yachtsman."

He chuckled softly. "Good answer. And the nicest thing anybody's said to me all day. All week, as a matter of fact. For that I think I'll let you stay." He touched her shoulder lightly. "Let's go over here and sit down. I not only missed dessert, but after-dinner drinks too. And it's always nice not to have to drink alone."

Delight flowed over her like the caress of a warm breeze with the sound of his amusement, the brief touch of his hand on her bare shoulder. He indicated a group of stationary deck chairs around a small table. The nearest chair was only a couple of steps away but Lanie felt distinct regret when he dropped his hand from her shoulder. And for more than one reason, as it turned out: the moment she turned toward the chairs the boat tilted against an unexpected swell and her feet slipped on the damp deck. Chris reached for her quickly but by that time she had already slid back against the guardrail, where she held on firmly.

"How long did you say it took to get your sea legs?" she inquired.

He smiled at the sight of her. "You should be okay soon." Then he glanced at her feet. "You're not wearing stockings, are you?"

"In small towns in the midwest," Lanie informed him, "ladies always wear stockings, or at least panty hose. Of course I am."

"Take them off."

Lanie stared at him.

"Take them off or go below. I mean it. Do you want to end up breaking your neck? Or falling overboard?"

"I promise I won't sue you."

But Chris was unmoved, and Lanie recognized a challenge when she saw it. He stood with his feet planted firmly apart, perfectly balanced against the motion of the ship, arms akimbo, and though his expression was not severe his tone made it very clear this was not a matter for debate as, Lanie imagined, very few of his orders would be. She also recognized when it was important not to back down.

Lanie let her shoes drop to the deck. Then, never taking her eyes from his, she reached beneath her skirt and began to wiggle out of her panty hose.

The jolt of surprise in his eyes gave her an enormous satisfaction, as did the amusement that quickly followed. And though her skirt kept her decently covered at all times Lanie knew the glint in his eye was due to more than admiration for her audacity, and she could not resist adding a particularly provocative wiggle or two to her striptease before she peeled the stockings off her feet. She held them up by the waistband for a moment for his inspection, then carefully wound them into a ball and stuffed them into a shoe.

Chris's eyes were dancing madly as he gestured toward a chair. "We may make a sailor out of you yet, Lanie Robinson. The first rule of good seamanship is to know how to take orders and you, if I may say so, do it exceptionally well."

"For now I'll take that as a compliment." Lanie moved, much more carefully this time, toward the lounger he indicated. She sat down and swung her feet up on the footrest. "The reason ladies from small towns in the midwest always wear stockings—no tan."

Chris found it impossible not to follow the contour of her legs as she spoke, and though he only caught a glimpse of their slender white form before she drew them up under her skirt, he found that glimpse startlingly exciting. Was it because she was trying so hard to cover them, or because he knew that underneath the skirt her legs were completely naked? He'd never given much consideration to what adorned a woman's legs before. But he would never again think of panty hose in the same way.

He took a bottle from the recessed holder in the center of the small table and splashed a measure into each of two glasses, passing one to her. "Cognac," he said. "Joel would be appalled, I'm sure, that it's being served in a plastic glass but that's another difference between sailing and yachting."

Lanie sniffed the contents cautiously. Even the aroma was fiery and intoxicating... not so very different from the man who served it, when she thought of it. "Umm," she murmured. "I really shouldn't drink so much." On a coquettish impulse she couldn't quite explain, she slanted a glance toward him and murmured, "Trying to get me drunk and have your way with me, are you?"

His returned gaze was frank and appreciative, but she did not miss the spark that had kindled low in his eyes. And he replied with a slight lift of his glass toward her, "My dear, if I wanted to have my way with you I wouldn't have to get you drunk."

Lanie found it much more difficult to break the eye contact than she had expected. "I can believe that," she said in a voice that was a little thicker, a little huskier than it should have been. She quickly took a sip of the brandy and managed in a more normal tone, "So why are we yachting instead of sailing?"

Chris slid down in the chair next to hers, his legs sprawled comfortably apart, his head resting on the chair back and his elbows propped up on the armrests as he balanced his glass on his abdomen. His arm brushed hers, a warmth that was more of a promise than a caress. She didn't move.

He answered, "New decorator, new crew, no time to supervise things myself. The *Serendipity* has always been a luxury cruiser, but until now no one ever accused it of being a floating palace. There's a microwave in the galley. Do you know how much power a microwave uses? And what about the water it takes to fill that fancy tub?" He sipped his brandy. "What's the point of leaving home if you bring home with you? Besides, with the amount of fuel we use and the weight of the supplies we're hauling, this boat is worthless for long voyages now."

"It's a beautiful boat, though," she replied.

"My grandfather built it. I could have done better."

Lanie stared at him. "Then why don't you?"

There seemed to be a bitter edge to his smile, but it might have just been the way the shadows fell. "I was too busy building the *Rendezvous*." And then, indicating her glass, "Don't you like the cognac? Would you rather have something else?"

What Lanie would rather have was coffee, and lots of it. The night was soft and rich and filled with too many teasing, tantalizing possibilities. Just sitting here beside him was intoxicating enough; she felt a strong need to keep her wits beside her.

"I'm sure it's very good," she answered. "But my head is already spinning." *And not entirely from the alcohol,* she thought, but did not say it aloud. "I'm afraid I'll get sick."

"On my boat? You wouldn't dare. The treatment for seasickness on board this vessel is keelhauling, on the theory that what doesn't kill you is bound to cure you."

"Sounds like a very good reason to stay sober to me."

His eyes twinkled in the dark. "Come on, loosen up. I can't grow a beard or tell dirty jokes—not tonight, anyway—so the least you can do is give me somebody to get drunk with."

She looked at him dubiously. "You're not an alcoholic, are you?"

He laughed. "No. And don't be too disappointed, Miss Small-Midwestern-Town, but I'm not a cokehead or a ruthless swindler or tax evader, either. I'm a little power-crazed, but other than that a perfectly normal thirty-six-year-old man—which only goes to prove that corporate giants are people too."

Lanie laughed. She *did* like him. "I think you're already a little drunk."

"Maybe." And he lifted his glass to her, smiling. "Maybe it's just the company."

She dropped her eyes to her own glass and took a small, cautious sip. It went down much more smoothly this time, but the glow lingered longer. "Thirty-six is awfully young to be head of a corporation. How did that happen?"

"My father died."

"Oh." She looked at him quickly. "I'm sorry."

"So was I." He took another sip from the glass, his eyes on the distant sea. "He died too young and I don't think I've ever quite forgiven him for it."

The silence that followed was brief and poignant and Lanie did not know how to fill it. She wasn't even sure she wanted to.

Then Chris looked at her, and invited easily, "So, tell me the Lanie Robinson story."

Lanie smiled into her glass. "Once upon a time..."

"Love it so far."

Lanie laughed a little, but when she glanced at him his expression was patient and interested, waiting for her to continue. She took another sip of her drink and resumed, a little more seriously. "Once upon a time in a typical suburban neighborhood in a typical small midwestern town lived a typical nuclear family— mom, dad, and three children, two girls and a boy. The oldest girl—that would be me—never had much of a childhood. My mother died when I was ten and my father was...well, never quite the same. My brother, Steve, was fifteen, and it was hard on him. Somebody had to pull the family together."

She shrugged, wondering if it was the brandy loosening her tongue, or the sympathetic ear of a stranger. Certainly the life she had left behind in Iowa was the last thing she wanted to talk about in this exotic shipboard paradise, but he had asked and it seemed perfectly natural to tell him.

"So while the other girls were going to the prom I was sewing ribbons on Cassie's—that's my younger sister—ballet slippers for her recital or making dinner while Dad worked late." A reluctant grin twisted the corner of her lips and she glanced at Chris askance. "I was a really ugly kid, too, so it's not as though I was turning down invitations by the dozen, either."

"That I don't believe." He sounded genuinely incredulous.

Over the years the mirror had grown kind to Lanie, but she never tired of hearing a genuine compliment like that, most particularly from a man like Chris. "I was though," she insisted. "All bones and angles, bad skin, bad hair..." Until two days ago, she had still had bad hair, and she touched the freshly shorn ends now as though for reassurance. "And my socks kept falling down. Did you go through a phase like that too?"

His voice was amused. "This is your story."

She tasted the brandy again. She was beginning to like it. "Well, I grew out of the Poor Lanie phase— eventually—and right into the Lanie Will Take Care of It phase. After high school I went on to the community college, planning to transfer my credits to the state university as soon as Cassie graduated and my dad didn't need me at home anymore. But by that time Steve was trying to start his construction business and he wasn't doing a very good job. Since I was the only one in the family who hadn't failed math I stepped in to straighten out his books, and by the time the business was on its feet my sister was in the middle of a divorce and needed someone to help her raise her two kids. I kept up with night classes for a while but gave up on the idea of transferring to the university."

"Cinderella, Cinderella," he murmured. "No Prince Charming?"

"If I ever did meet Prince Charming he'd probably want to borrow money." Lanie laughed. "No, I take that back, I did meet Prince Charming once. He borrowed my keys to pick up some ice cream for dinner. The police found him three days later trying to sell my car."

Chris groaned.

"And another time my brother fixed me up with one of his subcontractors—I mean, this guy could have been it. Good-looking, smart, fun to be with, and judging from what he charged our customers, he made a very good living. We had a great time together, until I invited him over for dinner one evening. He excused himself to freshen up, and I caught him in my bedroom, trying on my underwear. It was a little thing, I know, and I suppose I could have overlooked it but..."

Chris's eyes were brimming with laughter, his voice choked with it. "Please, no more. My God, where do you come up with these characters?"

"I can't tell you all my secrets." And she lifted one shoulder negligently. "Anyway, that's the Lanie Robinson story. Riveting, huh?"

"No happily ever after," Chris pointed out.

"I never even got to go to the ball." And then she leaned back in the chair, lifting her eyes to the sky. The clouds had an almost translucent look against the rich dark blue; Lanie had never seen anything like it. Watching that incredible forever sky with the boat rocking beneath her and the sea breeze on her skin was as much of an emotional experience as it was a sensual one. Like making love.

She said dreamily, "When I was young and dateless I used to absolutely devour the travel section of the Sunday paper. I'd clip all those articles about exotic adventures and romantic resorts, and I'd spend every free hour planning the trips I was going to take... Europe, India, Africa, floating down the Nile, cruising the Amazon, helicoptering in Alaska. And they weren't just daydreams, either. I planned budgets and itineraries and wardrobes and travel routes. It never occurred to me that there would ever be a single reason why I shouldn't go. Of course, a lot of things don't occur to you when you're young.''

For a moment Lanie let her thoughts travel back with wistfulness and regret. Lost dreams, lost youth. Then she realized how self-indulgent and prolonged the silence was becoming, and she lifted her glass again casually.

''So anyway, ten years later I'm still keeping my brother's books and still raising my sister's kids and I haven't ever, in my whole life, indulged any of my dreams. So a week ago I decided I'd had enough. I packed a bag, drove to Cedar Rapids, found a travel agent and here I am.'' And she glanced at him apologetically. ''Except that here, of course, is not where I'm supposed to be at all.''

''That,'' Chris said, saluting her with a small tilt of his glass, ''is the saddest story I've ever heard.'' He kept his tone light to disguise his true emotions, mostly because he didn't know what they were. Fascination was one of them. Admiration. And why he should feel either of those things for this woman he barely knew he could not say.

''Thank you. I can use all the pity I can get.'' And then she looked at him. ''Now your turn. Tell me the Chris Vandermere story.''

He leaned forward to pour more brandy into his glass. "Ah, a *real* fairy tale."

"I should expect so."

"Well, then." He leaned back, stretching out his long legs before him. "Prince Charming was born—"

Lanie laughed. "Is that who you are?"

"It's who I was meant to be, I assure you. Unfortunately life intervened, as it often does. If I may continue?"

"Please."

"I was born to wealth and privilege in a windswept, marble-halled mansion on Cape Cod, surrounded by water, surrounded by boats, attended by a virtual flock of uniformed nannies and butlers bearing silver trays."

"You're making that up."

He cocked an eyebrow at her. "My story, remember? Besides, I'm only exaggerating a little. I was raised surrounded by water and boats and weaned on stories of Great-Great-Grandpa Hannibal, who first came to these shores in the early eighteen-hundreds. He was a pirate."

Lanie looked at him. "Hannibal the pirate? Sounds wild."

"He was quite a character. He began his career—or I should probably say he advanced it—by smuggling goods to both sides during the War of 1812 and avoided the noose on more than one occasion with a combination of bribes, wits and sheer reckless bravado. I don't think he ever meant to be rich. Half his stunts were pulled for the sheer hell of it if you ask me. Or…" he glanced at her with a smile "…maybe just for the adventure. But whether he meant to or not, he's the one who started the shipping empire in this country. We're still the oldest privately owned shipping concern—what's left of us, that is. By the Civil War we were one of the most respected ship-builders in the nation. We sent the first troops to Europe during World War One, went into combat in World War Two. We've transported royalty and refugees, and materials that helped to build a nation or win a war. Now we're reduced to a fleet of party ships whose biggest battles are fought over which celebrities to sign for the New Year's cruise. I sometimes wonder what old Hannibal would think if he could see us now."

"So," Lanie observed thoughtfully, "that's why you come out here—sailing, instead of yachting. To try to recapture the spirit of Buccaneer Hannibal."

He looked surprised at her perception, and perhaps even a little uncomfortable. But then he smiled and raised his glass again. "Not bad, for an amateur."

"That's the story of the Holland-Alaska Cruise Line," she pointed out. "I haven't heard a thing about Chris Vandermere yet."

"Right. Sometimes it's hard to tell where one leaves off and the other begins."

He sipped his drink and the pause was so long that Lanie thought perhaps he had changed his mind and wouldn't continue. Then he said, "Like all fairy tales, my story is pretty predictable. Rich kid grows up to be rich young playboy—fast cars, fast women, yachting..." He glanced at her with a twinkle. "All charm and no substance, as my mother used to say, flash and style. I never had a serious thought in my head—in contrast to my little brother, Anthony, who was always kind of shy and introverted and awkward and probably would have been perfect for my job except for the fact that he's frankly not very bright. I was hardly the most qualified candidate to take over a company the size of Holland-Alaska, myself, but when my father, who neither sailed or yachted or, in fact, had taken a vacation since 1963, chose to have a heart attack at age fifty-two he left me his controlling share of the stock. So I had no choice but to take my rightful place behind the big desk and spend the rest of my life handing down decisions I was ill-prepared to make."

"You could have sold your stock," Lanie pointed out. "Or divided it with your brother or hired someone else to run the company."

"No, I couldn't."

"Why not?"

A crooked grin slid across his lips as he glanced at her. "Because I didn't want to. I'm power-crazed, remember? Besides, I had the weight of generations of tradition holding me down and that's not something you can just walk away from."

Lanie smiled slowly, looking down into her glass. "That's funny. No two people could be more different than we are, or have less in common, but we're both out here for the same reason."

"You're here," Chris pointed out, "because you got on the wrong boat."

"A technicality. What I mean is—"

"I know. We're both trying to escape from something. The same kinds of things, really. Responsibility, demands, pressures."

"The difference is of course that I came looking for the fairy tale and you've been living it all your life."

He smiled and extended his arm across the few inches that separated them, catching her hand. "Welcome to my fantasy."

The warmth of his hand around hers sent a startling tingle of pleasure through her that she couldn't quite disguise as her eyes met his. She saw a responsive softening in his own eyes and that confused her further. She looked away briefly.

"Thanks," she said, and managed a dismissive smile. "But I don't belong in your fantasy, and I don't think you're really very glad to have me."

"You're wrong."

He spoke quietly, and his thumb began to trace slow, tantalizingly erotic patterns over her palm beneath their linked fingers. Lanie looked at him, and his face was perfectly sincere, his eyes on their joined hands. Her heart sped its rhythm noticeably.

"I'm glad you got on the wrong boat," he said. "You've made a hard day end a lot more pleasantly than it would have otherwise and I thank you for that." He looked up at her. "I'm happy to have met you, Lanie Robinson, and I don't say that to many people."

Lanie knew she should withdraw her hand but she couldn't, not if her life had depended on it. The lazy circling caresses of his thumb sent waves of tingling sensation all the way up her arm, through her breasts, thickening her throat and making her voice husky.

"It's been a long day," she said. Very carefully, she leaned forward and put her glass into one of the indentations on the table. "I should get some sleep."

In tacit acknowledgment he ceased the caressing motions of his thumb. As she swung her feet to the deck he stood, placing his glass beside hers, and slipped his hands beneath her forearms to help her to her feet. The night was warm and Lanie's concentration was pleasantly fuzzy, but she was intensely aware of Chris's hands on her arms, of his closeness. This time it was not the motion of the boat that caused her to lose her balance but suddenly she found herself against his chest, his thighs pressing hers, his face so close that she could feel his breath like the caress of the sea breeze.

The moment seemed to stretch out forever. Sensation, expectation, suspended breath, sluggish heartbeat. His eyes moved slowly over her face, the color of moonlight on a deep, deep sea. Her hands rested against his chest as though for balance, though his grip upon her arms was firm. She could have pushed away. He could have stepped away. Neither of them moved.

He said, "You can use the main stateroom tonight. I'll sleep in the guest cabin."

His words seemed to have nothing to do with what was in his eyes. Yet some faraway part of her seemed to understand them, for she was surprised to hear her own voice reply, "No, I couldn't...."

He's going to kiss me, she thought. It shouldn't be, it couldn't be, but she was definitely in the arms of this exotic stranger, with the gentle rise and fall of the sea beneath her feet and the still night all around her. Even as her heart sped and her breath grew shallow in her throat there was a part of her that wasn't surprised at all, that had almost expected the night to end this way.

"You're the only woman on board," he said. "You should have your privacy."

But his eyes, moving over her like a stroking, lingering caress, left nothing about her private. She knew she should stop this, she should move away, say good-night while she still could.

But then he added softly, "If that's what you want."

Lanie held his gaze, her breath tight in her throat, a slow helpless fever tingling in her skin from the warmth of his hands. She said nothing.

Chris lifted his hand, tracing the curve of her cheekbone with the knuckle of his index finger. The very faintest hint of a smile curved his lips. "What did you really expect to find when you ran away, Lanie? Was it this?"

She ached for his kiss. His face was so close she could practically taste him. But it wasn't her mouth his lips touched; it was the curve of her neck, a slow hot tasting caressing of his tongue. The fever blossomed, took away her breath, weakened her knees.

"Or this?"

His fingers slipped beneath the strap of her sun-dress, lowering it off her shoulder. His tongue traced a pattern from the curve of her collarbone to her shoulder and then to the swell of her breast just where the material stopped. There his lips closed in a gentle drawing motion, his tongue circling, teasing.... Lanie thought her chest would explode with the thunder of her heart. The sky above her spun crazily. And never once had his hands left her arms, not once had his lips touched hers.

He lifted his face. She thought she could see a slight flush to his skin, and his eyes were as vast as the sky, deep and softly lit. The breeze ruffled his hair and teased her senses with the rich masculine scent of him: brine and brandy and memories of the sun.

He leaned very close to her so that his heat infused every pore; so close that his lips brushed hers when he spoke and she tasted, as well as heard, his words. "It's your fairy tale, Lanie Robinson. Tell me how it ends."

And just like that a world of possibilities began to unfurl before her, possibilities she had never even begun to consciously recognize before and yet they seemed perfectly reasonable, perfectly familiar. She, Lanie Robinson of Camden, Iowa, who had never had an adventure in her life, was on board a yacht in the middle of the Atlantic Ocean, being kissed in the dark by a tall handsome millionaire. Anything was possible. She, Lanie Robinson, who did not have sex with strangers, who never threw caution to the wind, who knew better than to take chances, suddenly could have anything she wanted.

And she wanted to savor it.

A slow soft smile touched her lips and she tightened her hands, ever so slightly against his chest. "I'll let you know," she said.

She turned to pick up her shoes and stockings, and found her own way below. She could feel him watching her, smiling in the dark, until she was out of sight.

Chapter Four

What would Grandpa Hannibal do?

Chris was a decisive man—he liked to think he had gotten that much from the gene pool of his heroic ancestors—and was for the most part accustomed to following his instincts, which was another way of saying that he did exactly what he wanted to. But when those instincts floundered he never went wrong by simply asking himself what his great-great-grandfather would have done.

It annoyed Chris to find his instincts in such conflict over Lanie Robinson. When it came to women he had *always* known what he wanted before. But on this occasion, wanting her was in direct conflict with the other thing he wanted almost as much.

Lanie Robinson was not the kind of woman he was accustomed to, which was probably exactly why she fascinated him so much. She was not shrewd or sophisticated or adept at playing chic little man-woman games. She was not the kind of woman he could enjoy and forget, and she had no place at all on the *Serendipity*.

He did not want to abandon her at the harbor to find her own way back to Iowa. As much as he tried not to admit it, the shadow of her spoiled vacation would hang over him like a thunderhead for the rest of the voyage. More importantly, he didn't want to go back to Miami at all.

This time alone on the *Serendipity* was more special to him than he would have liked anyone else to know. True, he needed the solitude, the change of pace. The way some men played golf or went to the gym every day, Chris sailed. The past had been enormously stressful, with the launch of the *Rendezvous* and all the attendant publicity, the dent in the cash flow, the decline of west coast operations. There had been times when the only thing that kept him from throwing up his hands and walking away from the whole thing was the thought of this voyage—that, and the almost certain knowledge that Madison would hunt him down with a machine gun and personally escort him back to the office where he belonged.

The real reason he needed this time so badly was much more elemental, and more private. The man and the sea, human skill versus the forces of nature, simple, uncomplicated, *necessary*. Those were battles as old as time, challenges as basic as the nature of man, and though they were battles Chris might not always win, at least he was comfortable in the arena. At least he understood the point. And if he made a mistake there was no time for regret; retribution was swift and final. For a few days, a week, a month—however much time he could steal from the jungles of civilization—he could come here and remember who he was. He could let the centuries slip away and walk the decks as Hannibal had done, hoist the sails and outrun the squalls as Hannibal had done, fight the battles against boredom and isolation and the solitude of his own thoughts in the same way his ancestor had done, and emerge a stronger man, ready to face the jungles again.

He needed that. And a woman—most especially a woman like Lanie Robinson—had no place in this part of his world.

But he didn't want to take her back.

His Grandpa Hannibal, Chris supposed, would have solved the dilemma by tying the interloper to a bedpost while he went about the ship's business, then visiting her at night until his lust was sated. That was an image Chris enjoyed for a good long while before finally dismissing it. While that idea did have a certain appeal, Chris doubted its practicality in this day and time. Not being the kind of man who belabored a question beyond all usefulness, he did not let the problem keep him awake. But he did fall asleep thinking of her.

When he awoke with the first faint light of dawn, completely rested and alert, the answer presented itself with perfect simplicity and clarity. And he thought it was a solution of which even Grandpa Hannibal would approve.

LANIE WAS AWAKENED in the middle of the night by a crack that was so loud she thought it was an explosion. Her feet were on the floor almost before the echo died, her heart roaring. She burst into the pilothouse, gasping and demanding of the figure at the helm, "What? What's wrong?"

Andrew glanced around with a smile and said pleasantly, "Morning, Miss Robinson. We didn't expect you up so early."

It was morning, Lanie realized dully as she looked through the spray-splotched windows at the dull gray sky and matching sea beyond. Barely morning, but morning nonetheless. "What was that noise?" she inquired breathlessly.

But his answer was superseded by another sharp crack, and Lanie lunged outside to see for herself.

The mainsail was raised and billowing with wind; Lanie was just in time to see Chris, with a deft maneuvering of ropes and pulleys, tie off a second, smaller sail—which Lanie fuzzily recalled from her reading on the plane might be referred to as the jib. Now both sails were filled and she could feel the increased velocity of the wind on her face as the boat picked up speed.

She braced her hand against the bulkhead for balance and shouted, "What's wrong? What was that noise?"

Chris turned, and for a moment Lanie's alarm faded and all she could think was, *My God. I can't believe I'm on a boat with a man who looks like that.* The morning air was chill, and he wore a navy windbreaker zipped over faded denim cut-off shorts. His rich chestnut hair was tossed wildly by the wind, and there was a shadow of beard on his lower jaw. The tendons in his legs were long and lean, flexed for balance against the motion of the ship, and his hands deft and strong as they made an intricate loop around a stanchion with absent, almost negligent grace. *All he needs,* Lanie reflected, somewhat dazzled, *is a sword in his belt and a gold earring and we could all step back in time a couple of centuries. . . .*

He gave her a lazy morning grin and replied, "That was the sails, filling with air. I like to start off with a bang."

How could she have forgotten that grin, those hands, the subtle power in that long-lined body... particularly since she had spent most of the night dreaming of nothing else? Just looking at him brought back a flood of sensations and slow spreading warmth that, for the moment at least, left her completely oblivious to the morning temperature.

She was suddenly acutely aware of her own disheveled appearance—her rumpled hair, the plain cotton nightshirt that barely reached the middle of her thighs, her face devoid of makeup. Beneath the easy caress of his grin she felt distinctly disadvantaged. She wasn't certain that the gooseflesh on her arms was from the chill of the air, and she rubbed her arms self-consciously. And as his gaze swept over her, heating her skin, she felt the cooling effects of the breeze and shivered, rubbing one foot against the opposite ankle to warm it.

"It's the middle of the night!" she protested.

"Only to a landlubber." He secured a length of rope and came toward her with that easy rolling stride she had already begun to associate with him. "You're just in time for one of the most spectacular sights you'll ever know—sunrise at sea."

She shivered again. "I've never seen a sunrise in my life and I'd prefer not to break my record, thank you. How long before we dock?"

"I'm glad you brought that up."

She had turned to go back inside, now she stopped and looked back at him curiously. The expression on his face was difficult to read, particularly at that hour of the morning and in the pre-dawn light. "Oh?"

"Yes." He rested one hand against the bulkhead of the pilothouse at shoulder level, looking down at her. His eyes were a mirror of the sea and had taken on the secret gray depths of the morning that surrounded them. "I've been giving your situation some thought."

Lanie ran her fingers through her hair uneasily, wishing she had taken the time to look in a mirror before she ran out of the cabin, and then realizing how ridiculous that was. "My situation?"

He nodded. "What are you planning to do when you get back to Miami?"

There was a depressing thought. She had gone to sleep in the middle of a fairy tale, and had awakened to find reality had never been so cruel. Do? What could she possibly be expected to do? She had the return half of a round-trip ticket to Iowa, a credit card that was over the limit, a hundred dollars in traveler's checks and a handful of small bills for tips. She did not have a great deal of choice.

She lifted her shoulders, aiming for nonchalance, but let them drop heavily. "With any luck, I'll be able to find out what happened to my luggage. And maybe exchange my ticket home for an earlier date without too much of a penalty. I certainly can't afford to stay in Miami until the next cruise leaves."

"There's an island about three sailing days away called Player's Cay," Chris said. "The cruise line owns it. Our seven- and fourteen-day cruises disembark there once a voyage for picnicking, snorkeling, that kind of thing. We planned to make a provisioning stop there ourselves, and as it happens, the *Rendezvous* is scheduled to stop that same day. I've spoken with the captain and he says there'll be no problem taking you aboard for the remainder of the cruise. If you're interested, of course."

Lanie stared at him. "Ten days on the most luxurious cruise ship afloat and you want to know if I'm *interested?*"

He nodded.

Lanie stared at him for a moment longer, then turned her gaze toward the sea, where the faintest streaks of pink and yellow were beginning to appear on the horizon. She thought again about fairy tales.

She looked at him. "I can't afford a cruise on the *Rendezvous.*"

"We'll work out some kind of transfer from your other cruise."

She said skeptically, "I don't see how you're going to be able to do that."

"That's my problem." Then he smiled. "Look, I can't take you to the ball, but every girl deserves to live at least one dream in her life."

If only he hadn't smiled. She was quite sure she would have been able to view the entire situation much more rationally if only he hadn't smiled. Not that she ever had any intention of turning him down. But when that smile went through her, it was with a slow meltdown of every important nerve relay in her body and it was very hard to maintain any dignity at all.

She said softly, "I thought you said you weren't a nice guy."

The smile deepened. "I lied."

Lanie had to look away. Everything inside her was leaping and jumping and turning cartwheels for joy and it was very hard to maintain any semblance of nonchalance at all. When she saw the first glimmer of gold begin to shimmer off the distant sea, backlighting the sky with shades of fuchsia and lemon, she could no longer restrain a smile. "What do you know?" she murmured. "Sunrise."

Then she turned to him. "I accept your generous invitation. But I want to know something first."

"I hope it doesn't have anything to do with money, because I really can't allow you to pay."

"Good, because I wasn't going to offer." This time she managed to ignore the twinkle that came into his eyes, mimicking the play of the sun on water. "What I want to know is..." she drew a breath "...does this have anything to do with what happened between us last night?"

His gaze never wavered, and the light play, if possible, only deepened in his eyes. Lanie's body responded to the teasing, playful caress of his gaze as though to the touch of his hand. He said, "I don't know. Does it?"

Lanie's lips tightened at the corners as her own smile deepened, and she met his eyes boldly. "Maybe," she replied. "But I think the real reason is that you just don't want to turn back for Miami."

He burst into laughter. "That's what I like about you, Lanie Robinson. A woman of perception *and* few words."

"That's really very manipulative of you, you know. Dangling a prize under my nose that I can't possibly refuse."

"Manipulation has always been one of my best things."

"Fortunately for you, I'm an easy mark."

"Right." He grinned. "Now go below and get some chow. Today we do some serious sailing."

Lanie managed to keep a look of pleasant composure on her face until she reached the pilothouse, and Andrew must have thought she had lost her mind when the big grin split her face. She balled her hands into power fists and exclaimed triumphantly under her breath, *"Yes!"*

Three more days with Chris. The *Rendezvous* waiting. Nassau, the Grand Caymens. Three more days with Chris. Life was good. Life was perfect. And she wouldn't have traded her fantasy for all the glass slippers in the world.

WHEN SUNSET FINALLY CAME Lanie collapsed in a deck chair scrubbing the zinc oxide off her nose and running her fingers through her limp bedraggled hair. She pushed her sunglasses up into her hair and let her eyes close against the sparks of dying sunlight that danced on her lids. When she felt Chris's shadow fall over her she did not even open her eyes.

"I have something to tell you," she said. "I hate sailing. A lot."

Sailing, she had discovered, consisted mostly of brassy sunshine, stinging spray, slippery decks and aching muscles. Sailing was hard work. Her head was filled with a jumble of nonsensical terms like halyards and boltrope, reeve the jib sheets and flying jibe and beam reaching and she frankly did not care if she ever tied another knot again.

There was amusement in Chris's tone as he sat down in the chair beside her. "Good thing this isn't going to be a long-term relationship then."

Almost, she was persuaded to open her eyes. "And I want you to know that while I appreciate your wanting to share with me the thrill of getting sweaty and windblown and almost brained by the mast—"

"Boom," Chris corrected. "The mast is what holds the sails upright."

"I'd appreciate it even more," Lanie continued unperturbed, "if you wouldn't share with me anymore."

"But look at it this way." The undertone of laughter in Chris's voice was clear. "If I get swept overboard and Andrew and Joel both come down with a debilitating case of salmonella, you now know how to sail the boat to safety."

"Ha! I know how to sail the boat right into an oil tanker."

The laughter broke through in the form of a chuckle, lazy and relaxed. "You're the one who wanted to try something new, remember?"

"Yes, thank you very much, I do. Now I want a long, long nap."

"How about a beer first?"

She opened her eyes and sat up a little straighter as she took a bottle. First she held it against her forehead, cooling it, then her cheeks, then her throat, trailing droplets of moisture along her skin. The subtle light in Chris's eyes as he watched her was what she had been looking for all day. It was almost worth what she had endured to see it now.

Subduing a secret smile, she drank from the bottle, watching as Chris did the same. He sat comfortably slumped in that way he had, knees apart, feet tucked beneath the chair. The denim cutoffs stopped high on his thighs, below them his legs were strong and golden tanned, hairs glinting reddish gold in the late-afternoon light. He had shaved, after all, but his hair was a riot of wind-tossed layers and rich autumn colors. She couldn't look at his hair without imagining what it would feel like, gathered by the handful between her fingers. A chambray shirt, splotched with spray and perspiration, was open over his bare chest, and not for the first time that day Lanie's heart began to speed from no more than simply looking at him. Try as she might, she could not imagine this vital, elemental man sitting behind a desk in a shirt and tie, conducting board meetings and reviewing stock options. Or if he was, she could not imagine him being any good at it.

The very notion brought a puzzled smile to her lips, and she shook her head.

"What?" Chris asked.

"I was just thinking..." She slid her gaze toward him lazily. "What would you be doing now in the real world?"

"You sure know how to break a mood, don't you? What would you be doing?"

Lanie winced. "I see what you mean." She took another thoughtful sip of her beer, surprised by how hard it was to place herself back in the life she had left behind. It was as though more than a couple of days and a few thousand miles separated then from now; it was almost as though that life belonged to someone else entirely.

She said, "I guess right about now I'd be trying to decide whether to make tuna casserole or tacos for dinner, Beth would be screaming that someone had used her hair dryer, Brian would be blasting that awful heavy-metal music from his room, and about that time Cassie would call to say she has to work late.... Please, your turn. I'm depressing myself."

"That doesn't mean I have to do the same."

Lanie said softly, "Just look at that sky."

It was no wonder she found it easy to forget what she had left behind when the here and now was so compelling, so breathtaking. The sun hovered on the horizon like a shiny coin, spilling its brassy reflection into the waters below. The sky was a rich twilight blue, almost indigo, streaked with brilliant orange and deep yellow and fiery alizarin. The ocean surged and fell, shimmering with light, a succession of gently rolling swells flecked with foam. In the distance a seagull dived, and closer to the boat a playful sea creature jumped and splashed. Lanie sighed.

"I take it back," she murmured. "I love sailing."

But Chris wasn't watching the sunset or the sea, even though they both continued to thrill him no matter how many times he had seen them in all their many moods. He was watching Lanie. Her face was kissed with the sun, her eyes as bright as cellophane, and it was as though he had never seen a sunset before seeing it reflected in her eyes.

"I guess it does beat tuna casserole and heavy metal," he said.

Still holding him with that gentle, brighter than light gaze, she said, "I don't know how you can ever bear to go back."

"It's hard, sometimes," he admitted. He let his hand slide to the back of her neck, caressing it briefly, then across her shoulder and down her arm, where his fingers linked with hers in an easy natural way. He turned her hand over in his, studying it, admiring it, enjoying how nicely it fit into his when he closed his fingers around it.

Then he smiled and looked at her, just because he wanted to see her smile back. He leaned back in his chair, their fingers linked loosely between them, and added, "But it's a job, and somebody has to do it."

Lanie laughed softly, throatily. "I'm sure." She looked at him curiously. "So what would you do if you didn't have that job? If you could do anything else in the world."

"First," Chris replied immediately, "I'd take about a year off and sail around the world. Maybe longer, as long as it took to see everything I want to see and do everything I want to do. And when I was ready to set-

tle down I'd start my own business, doing what I want
to do.''

''Which is?''

He drank from the bottle. ''Building ships. Not like
the *Rendezvous*, which wasn't a ship as much as a hotel and which I didn't build at all, but sailboats and sail
cruisers, yachts—the vessels that really get wet, that
test the designer's skill and courage, that provide the
forum for real cutting-edge innovation, right down
there at sea level where it matters. That's what I'd do.''

His answer didn't surprise Lanie, but his passion
did. She would not have imagined that a man like
Chris, who had so much more than most people even
dreamed of, who controlled his own destiny as deftly
as he manipulated the wind, could want anything with
very much conviction. But she could feel his excitement as he spoke, in the tone of his voice, in the slight
tightening of his fingers around hers, and see it in the
pleased, determined look that came into his eyes as he
gazed at the distant horizon, as though somewhere out
there one of his proudest designs had just sailed into
view.

''I don't understand,'' she said. ''Why don't you?''

He glanced back at her. ''No time,'' he replied, and
lifted the bottle to his lips a final time. He looked at
her again and added more honestly, ''No guts.''

But before Lanie could pursue that, he asked,
''What about you? What would you rather do than

keep your brother's books and raise your sister's children?''

She laughed. ''Almost anything.''

''I'm serious.''

She opened her mouth to reply but was stopped by sudden, unaccustomed shyness. She took a quick sip of her beer to hide it. ''This is a silly conversation.''

''That's what sailing is for. Quiet contemplation, long meditations, silly conversations. Tell me.''

''You'll think it's dumb.''

''Now I've got to know.''

She hesitated, but the warmth of his hand around hers felt so good and his expression was so open and relaxed, that almost before she knew it she was confiding, ''An astronomer. I've always wanted to be an astronomer. I don't know anything about it except what little the local library has and what I've seen on public television, and I gave my nephew a telescope once for his birthday. But I've always kind of pictured myself traveling to the desert outback to watch a total eclipse of the moon at its apogee, or to the south pole to study the Pleiades or...'' and she glanced at him shyly ''...on ship in the middle of the ocean somewhere tracing the path of a comet.

''Of course...'' She shrugged. ''I know that most of an astronomer's life is spent hunched over a computer or a radio printout, but I don't care.'' Despite her best efforts, her voice grew dreamy again. ''Just studying what's out there, just working with the stars...every day would be a surprise. Anything could happen, I'd always be learning something new, and— I don't know, it would just make me feel connected, somehow to...possibilities." Again she glanced at him, this time apologetically and somewhat self-consciously. "I told you it was silly."

But he was smiling, and the depth of his smile caused a surprised flush of warmth to go through her. "Why don't you?"

The brilliance of the sunset played in his eyes just as it did on the water. It was hard to look away from his eyes, or to concentrate on much of anything at all with his smile warming her, his thumb gently, almost absently massaging the sensitive area of her inner wrist, just over her pulse. He had strong hands, but soft. An artist's hands. Or a lover's.

She said, confused, "What?"

"Why don't you become an astronomer?"

"Oh, sure. Right." She took a final sip from the bottle and put it on the table. "I'm almost thirty-five years old, I don't quite have two years of college, and I should run off and become an astronomer."

"You know what they say. It's never too late."

She laughed.

"Besides, you ran off and stole aboard my boat, didn't you? Seems to me it would just be a matter of moving from one fantasy to another."

Gently, Lanie withdrew her hand and swung her feet to the deck, keeping her tone light. ''There are certain things in this world you can have, and certain things you can't. The trick is to know the difference—fantasies notwithstanding. And a glamorous life as an astronomer simply isn't in the stars for me. So to speak.'' And with an apologetic glance at him for the pun, she got up and walked to the rail.

The deepest, richest hour of sunset was upon them now as the brilliant colors began to fade into pastel and were absorbed by the violet sky. The ocean was rippled with silver and shot through with a deep black-green and just above the horizon, glowing faintly, the evening star appeared. Venus, for lovers. Lanie smiled secretly. It was fairy-tale perfect.

Chris came to stand beside her. The awareness that stirred between them was an electric thing, undisguised and unrestrained. Did he read her thoughts, or did he have to even try? Hadn't she been telegraphing her feelings in every movement, every glance, every time he was near?

Her heart picked up its rhythm, her skin prickled with his nearness. One hand slid around her waist, turning her gently to face him. When she did she felt the brush of his naked thighs against the sun-warmed flesh of her own, and her heart began to pound with anticipation and certainty. She looked up at him, and except for the low, knowing light in his eyes his expression was perfectly ordinary, his tone conversational.

"Let's talk about some of the things you can have," he said. Lanie lifted her hands to his face, cupping it, feeling the slightly rough texture of his skin beneath her fingers, drawing him close. Her heartbeat was a cascade now of fear and excitement and certainty. *Just once,* she thought. And before she lost her courage, she leaned forward, drawing him closer, and kissed his mouth.

Just once. Just a taste. Just a moment to indulge the fantasy, to pretend the fairy tale could come true. That was all she wanted, all she expected . . . yet she knew from the moment her lips touched his it would not end there. Nor had she ever wanted it to. As inevitably as drawing a breath, the passion flared between them and she felt herself sinking into it, weak and dizzy and drowning within it. His mouth opened beneath hers, tasting her as she tasted him, bold and plundering, and his hands tightened on her waist, steadying her, even as her hands plunged into his hair, cupping his scalp. His hands slid down, long fingers cupping her buttocks, holding her close as he pushed one thigh between hers, exerting a slow unerring pressure upward.

Sensation exploded within her, and her moan was lost in his mouth just as her will and her reason were lost in the feverish swell of sharp-edged pleasure that was consuming her body.

His hands moved up, shaping her waist and her back, and his leg shifted slightly so that his pelvis was against hers, and she could feel the heat and the power of his arousal. His face was flushed, his eyes luminous in the fading light, and his breathing as uneven as her own even though he tried to control it. "So tell me," he demanded softly, holding her arms. "Tell me what you want."

Lanie tried to look away and couldn't. She wanted to lie to him but didn't know how to begin. Her hands drifted down to his shoulders, then slid around his neck. His skin was smooth and hot and damp beneath his hair. She wanted to draw him close, to taste him again.

She said, as steadily as she could, "There are certain rules for women like me. We don't turn our backs on responsibility to go chasing after wild daydreams...."

His lips touched the corner of her left eye, forcing her eyes to close as a ripple of pleasure went through her.

"Of course not."

She drew an uneven breath. "We don't belive in fairy tales."

"Good for you."

His tongue swept across the curve of her neck between her earlobe and collar bone. Her fingers tightened on the back of his neck as the sensation washed through her, making her knees weak.

"We don't," she said steadily, "have sex with strangers. That would be reckless and stupid."

Chris lifted his face to look at her. His fingers traced the curve of her cheekbone with a touch as light as the caress of a sea breeze. "It would only be reckless and stupid if we were." He took one of her hands in his, bringing her fingers to his lips. "Am I such a stranger, Lanie?" he asked softly.

A stranger? How could he be a stranger? He had lived inside her little-girl's dreams for as long as she could remember. He was the reason tales were spun and songs were sung, the gallant young hero who had been seducing maidens with whispered promises of happily-ever-after since the beginning of time. He was that one wild moment every woman lives for, the memory she would look back upon with fond regret for the rest of her life, and if Lanie turned her back on him now she would never forgive herself.

His face filled her vision, his hair gently tossed by the wind, his eyes as deep as the bottom of the sea. She said softly, "Sometimes . . . rules were made to be broken."

Chapter Five

He literally swept her off her feet. Outside the main cabin he lifted her in his arms and carried her over the threshold like a princess bride and Lanie thought dizzily that no one had ever done that for her. The wall lamps illuminated the room softly, and one part of Lanie's mind noted with dim surprise that the bed had been turned down. He laid her against the pillows and it was like floating on air, as though her arms and legs—indeed, her whole body—didn't even belong to her, as though this were some strange and beautiful erotic dream.

But it wasn't a dream, and that was the best part. He knelt astride her, the warmth of his body falling over her, his face intent and his eyes alive as they moved over her face, her throat, her breasts, making her breathing faster, making her chest ache just from the power of his gaze. And then he slipped his hands beneath the material of her shirt and drew it up and over her head. Her heart began its shattering, pounding rhythm, and when he reached to undo the front clasp of her bra, slipping the straps from her shoulders, she was sure he could feel it. He sat back on his heels, not touching her, not kissing her, just looking at her.

The sight of her dark hair tumbled on his pillow was intoxicating, her petal-white skin, the soft full swell of her breasts, those big soul-drinking eyes, now fever bright... Just the touch of those eyes could set his skin on fire. He had wanted before, yet never with this swiftness, this intensity, this *importance*. Lanie was different, and the most disturbing thing was that he did not completely understand why.

He wanted her, all of her, with a fierce possessive need that surprised him with its power, and he wanted her to want him with that same knife-edged ache. But more, he wanted to fill her need, he wanted to show her pleasure she had never guessed at before, to be for her what no man had ever been and give to her what no one had ever given before.

Lanie lifted her hands, wanting to touch his face, his hair, his chest, to somehow break the spell of suspended wanting in which he had entrapped her. But he caught her hands in both of his and brought them to his lips. He drew his tongue across the knuckles of her closed hands, and then his teeth. Then he stretched her arms out on either side of her, holding them, as he lowered himself over her. He kissed her stomach, just where the waistband of her shorts began. She gasped as his tongue traced a slow, heated pattern up the center line of her body and then across. His mouth covered her breast.

Her fingers tightened against the gentle restraint of his as she writhed with the pleasure he created, slow heated waves of need that swelled from the magic his mouth worked on her breasts to the very core of her womb. And just when she thought she'd cry out with the intensity of the sensation, his mouth moved upward, covering hers. His hands opened on hers, moving slowly, deliberately, over the length of her arms, pressing into the swell of her torso, sliding downward with exquisite, almost reverent slowness to her waist. Her skin had become a web of tactile receptors that was activated solely by his touch, and each caress, each whisper of his breath across her heated flesh sent off a series of small explosions in the center of her brain. She was on fire.

She thrust her hands beneath his open shirt and arched upward until she tasted the smooth honey skin of his chest against her tongue. She pushed his shirt off his shoulders and freed his arms from the sleeves; she kissed his collarbone and his shoulder and the hot, damp hollow of his throat. He tasted of sunshine and salt. Her hands explored the breadth of his back, the long taut muscles and heated skin. She drew him close, sinking back against the pillows, pushing her hands into his hair as she sought his mouth again. And she thought, *Too good to be true...*

His length stretched over her for a moment, covering her with his weight, his chest pressing her breasts, heat blending, flesh fusing. And then he drew away, sitting up slowly, and Lanie's heart pounded a confused anxious rhythm with the absence of him. He slipped his fingers inside the waistband of her shorts, working the first button, then the second, his fingertips brushing against the tightening flesh of her lower abdomen, across the elastic band of her bikini panties. Anticipation pounded within her, coiled like a spring ready to break. The third button opened, and the last. His fingertips brushed over the gentle mound of her sex and she gasped with the sensation, her hands convulsing on his arms. Then his hand moved upward, opening across her bare abdomen, pressing against the ache of desire that knotted within her. He lowered his head and pressed a kiss into her flesh, just below her navel, his circling tongue sending a surprising rush of fullness and liquid heat to the apex of her thighs.

He caught the open edges of her shorts, slipping his fingers beneath the elastic of her panties, and tugged both garments down over her hips. Sitting up, he slid the material down her legs and off her feet, then gently arranged her legs on either side of him, tracing the length of her legs with slow, long caresses. Her calves and her knees and her lower thighs were still slippery with sunscreen and his hands glided over her oiled flesh, slow long sensuous strokes that moved ever closer to, but never quite touching, the center of her desire. The muscles of her thighs ached and quivered, straining against his gentle hold, but she was not sure whether it was in an effort to draw away or to pull closer.

She moaned out loud and reached for him, arching against him, her grasping fingers brushing only his arms. Yet he came to her, slipping his hands beneath her, caressing her buttocks and her back as his chest, heated and slick with perspiration, slid against hers. His breath mingled with hers, deep and controlled yet uneven at the edges, his heartbeat like an anvil hammer, the force of which was barely distinguishable from her own. She could feel his power, his hardness through the denim material as he pressed against her and she arched greedily into him as his mouth covered hers.

He moved away from her and she felt an acute stab of alarm, but through the fog of passion and need she could hear the sounds of his undressing, see him only an arm's length out of reach.

He returned to her, taking her outstretched arms in his hands, holding them still as he moved between her knees. Her heart was pounding with uncertainty, an-

ticipation and a little fear as he placed her hands over
her head and left them there, sitting back. His fingertips stroked a light tantalizing pattern from her ankle
to her inner thigh and his eyes were mesmeric in the
dark, watching her, pinning her beneath their power.

He slid his hand beneath her knee, lifting it slightly,
turning to trace the path his fingers had followed with
his tongue. Lanie went very still, every fiber of her
being focused on the electric sensation that spiraled
upward, tightening into aching, maddening need. He
pressed a kiss deep into the crease where thigh met
torso, and then his tongue flicked caressingly, explor-
ingly, over the center of her sex and she thought she
would explode with the intensity of the sensation.

She tried to pull away, gasping as she arched her
back into the mattress, but his fingers tightened on her
thighs, holding her still. She was helpless against the
maddening darts of his tongue, the electric jolts of
sensation that burst through her, and her gasp turned
into a muffled moan, and then a cry of need so intense, of pleasure so shocking, it was almost painful.
His tongue moved in tight circles, his lips caressed, his
teeth teased, and when she thought she could not en-
dure any more, he eased his attentions, only to return
in another second with more intensity, for he knew the
secrets of her deepest pleasure and he knew how to
plunder it. Lanie tossed her head on the damp pillow,
her fingers clutching at the sheets, and when she cried

out his name she thought he would stop; she knew she would die if he stopped. He pushed her to the edge, and then beyond, and when the cascades of pleasure began they were endless, tumbling, an avalanche that gained force and substance as it descended.

The spasms of gasping, helpless delight seemed to go all the way to her thighs; they left her sobbing for breath, clinging to Chris, dazed and drenched with sweat. She saw the blur of his face, the dark light source that was his eyes as he kissed the perspiration from her cheeks, her eyes. Her head dropped back weakly against the crook of his arm and his lips pressed into the arch of her throat, pressing into the fast, hard throb of her pulse as though he could take her very heartbeat into himself. She felt his thighs separating hers, his hardness poised against her still swollen, aching flesh, and a small moan of protest formed low in her throat because she thought she couldn't, not so soon, not again. And then his hands cupped her face, making her look at him, and she opened her eyes to his face above her, strong and beautiful, eyes that seemed to hold all the power of the night and all the mystery of the sea. She wanted him, she wanted the pleasure he could give and the pleasure she could give him. Her arms went around him, her mouth lifted to his even as her hips arched, drawing him inside her.

It was a slow, exquisite filling and every fiber of her being was suffused in the sensation, for it was more than pleasure, this intimacy, this knowing of the size and shape of him and taking him into her body, making him a part of her.... This strangeness, this wonder. For he was more than a half-formed dream, more than a fantasy lover now. He was Chris. And he was very real.

When he began to withdraw from her she cried out loud and instinctively grasped his shoulders, but he remained poised against her and filled her again, only this time thrusting deeper. Her head spun. The thrusts came faster, and she rose to meet them. Control slipped away as the intensity built, and she lost all conscious thought, all reason, all ability to care about or recognize anything except the pleasure that was building inside her. She did not know what she had expected but it had never been as complete as this, absorbing every particle of her mind and body and will into this man...her lover, the answer to her emptiness, the only dream she had ever had that had come true. And, for this moment and as long as it lasted, hers alone.

The release was explosive, blinding, shattering and it seemed to last forever. Dimly she felt the shudders rack his body as she clung to him, gasping, tasting him on her tongue as her open mouth pressed into his shoulder. They collapsed together, exhausted and dazed, and it was a long time before Lanie was aware of anything except his heartbeat and hers and the simple, mindless presence of what they had just shared.

LANIE MUST HAVE DOZED, because when she felt the brush of Chris's hand on her shoulder she was surprised to see him sitting on the bed beside her, gently drawing the sheet over her perspiration-cooled body. "Don't wake up," he said softly. "I like watching you sleep."

With a wordless murmur, Lanie smiled and lifted her hand to caress his arm. "How long?"

"Just a few minutes."

He had not put on his clothes, and Lanie realized this was the first time she had actually looked at him fully naked. The strong flow of his chest into lean waist, the patches of dark reddish hair beneath his arms and low on his body, the shape of his sex. His thighs, his strong firm calves. His hands, his long magical fingers, the column of his throat and the breadth of his shoulders and the lean muscles of his arms. Lanie would have thought it was impossible, but she was growing aroused just looking at him.

And the wonderful thing about being lovers was that he could see it in her eyes, without her having said a word. And she could see the answering smile in his. She murmured, "What time is it?"

He wrapped a lock of her hair around his finger, his eyes twinkling. "Do you have an appointment?"

She let her hand trail down his arm, lightly, lazily, caressing his ribcage, drifting over his hip and resting at last atop his thigh. She could see the low responsive light in his eyes. But the beautiful thing about being lovers was that anticipation could be savored, the urgency subdued, and time was on their side.

"I just don't want to be late for dinner."

The smile in his eyes deepened to surprised amusement. "The refrigerator is well-stocked if you're hungry." He lifted the glass of mineral water he held in one hand as evidence. "Do you want me to bring you something? Or I could tell Joel to serve dinner now if you like." And he winked at her. "This cruise line also provides room service, you know."

She shook her head quickly and adamantly. "Oh, no. I don't want them to think—that is, it's a small boat and if we're late for dinner or anything they might think..."

"That we found something better to do?" His eyes were twinkling madly now.

She nodded uncomfortably.

He burst into laughter. "You *are* a funny lady." He set the glass aside and, propping his arms on either side of her pillow, leaned forward to drop a kiss on her forehead. "What possible difference can it make?"

The brush of his lips, the blanket of his heat, the scent of him and the nearness of him set off an avalanche of sensory impressions that made it very difficult to concentrate on the subject at hand, and even more difficult to be annoyed with him. Her hands drifted over his arms in long smooth strokes even as she tried to make her voice stern. "It makes a difference to me. Maybe you're accustomed to ignoring the servants but I'm not. It would embarrass me to think they knew I was sleeping with the captain."

"They're not servants, they're crew." He placed a kiss, slow and tender, just beneath the curve of her cheekbone. "And if either one of them did or said anything to embarrass you I'd hang him from the nearest yardarm."

Her hands slid around his waist, stroking his back. Her foot caressed his ankle as he stretched over her. "I'm serious."

His hands cupped her face; his eyes, so very close to hers, were as soft as nighttime, as rich as Christmas velvet. He said, "So am I."

Wonderful familiarity, sweet, rich comfort. His touch, his smile, his slightest caress were filled with the quiet certainty of newfound intimacy, yet laced with the excitement of its newness, the promise, the promise of wonders yet to be discovered. Lanie looked into his eyes, into his strong beautiful face and she could not believe this was happening to her. That it was him, that it was her, that the lovemaking they had just shared was not simply a dream from which she might soon awake. His body covered hers now, awakening every nerve fiber, stirring inside her a depth of desire she did not think she was capable of feeling again so soon.

She said thickly, "This is not the conversation I want to be having now."

He rested his weight on his forearms, his hands framing her face as one thumb gently stroked her cheek. She could feel his arousal against her stomach. His smile drifted over her and through her, as rich as a sea breeze, as heady as strong wine. "What do you want to talk about?" he asked.

There were a dozen things she wanted to tell him, a hundred. How he was the first perfect thing that had ever happened to her in her entire life. How even in her wildest dreams she could not have summoned up a man like him and even if she had she never would have dreamed that making love with him could be so wonderful. That, if nothing else happened to her for the rest of her life, she would be content for having known him, for having been allowed to pretend, for even a little while, that what they shared was real.

But even as she tried to form the words they sounded heavy-handed, self-important, an intrusion into this magical moment. She lifted his hands, threading her fingers through his hair, adoring the silky, slightly damp texture of it, entranced by the way it sifted through her fingers. "Do you know something?" she said softly. "You're the most fun I've ever had."

She shifted beneath him, encircling him with her arms and legs, drawing him into her with a long slow shivery breath of sensation so intense she could hardly contain it. She closed her eyes and held him close and let the dream spin out.

CHRIS HELD HER in the circle of his arms, touching his lips lightly to her hair, and some distantly amazed part of his mind observed that for the first time in his life he understood those who said that the afterglow was almost as sweet as the act itself.

He didn't want to move. He didn't want to talk, or sleep or drink or eat or think. He wanted nothing more, for now and always, than what he held in his arms. Such complete and thorough contentment was a rare thing for Chris. He wasn't sure in fact that he had ever felt it at all.

He didn't know why making love with Lanie was so different from anything he had known before. Perhaps it was because Lanie herself was so different from any woman he had ever known, perhaps because when he was with her *he* felt different. That frightened him a little.

He had started out wanting nothing but to give her pleasure. But what had begun as an act of skill had soon ceased to be a performance. Perhaps because her response to him was so guileless and spontaneous, perhaps because simply being with her, in bed or out, was so artless, so effortless, so constantly, completely natural that technique was forgotten, style disappeared and almost before he knew it he felt himself being drawn into the essence of what was simply Lanie.

It was as though until Lanie he had been making love with only half his attention, half his senses. It was like seeing in black and white all his life and suddenly opening his eyes to color. It was more than sex; it was all of her.

And that was what confused him.

She stirred in his arms and he bent his head to hers, combing her hair away from her face with his fingers. "Okay?" he inquired softly.

She nodded against his shoulder. He could feel the curve of her smile. "I feel so sinful you wouldn't believe."

He chuckled, low in his throat. "Not the answer I expected, but I can live with it."

And then he had to ask. He caught her chin lightly with two fingers and tilted her face to look at him. "Regrets?"

Her smile was sleepy and sated. Her fingers caressed his face. "Oh, yes," she said. Her fingertips trailed over his throat, a little dance of light and sensation. "Enough to last a lifetime. That's the best part."

It was a joke, and he smiled, but he realized with a sudden surprising intensity that he didn't want her to feel regrets. Not for a moment. Not even in jest.

But he did not know how to tell her that, nor even if he wanted to. So he kissed her lips lightly and he said, "You've got twenty minutes to dress for dinner. And I wouldn't have told you that except that I think it's important that you keep up your energy." He grinned at the playful twinkle that came into her eye and placed another kiss on the corner of her eyebrow. "And because I did something stupid. I told Andrew I'd take first watch tonight." With one last regretful taste of her lips, he sat up.

Her disappointment was obvious. "Do you mean now? You're not even going to eat?"

He was more pleased by her reaction than he should have been, and for a moment even considered having Joel take his watch. That was what he paid him for, after all. Chris had never missed a watch before. For any reason.

The very fact that he was tempted disturbed him more than he wanted to admit, and he had to force casualness into his tone as he swung his feet to the floor. "I'll have something later. And unless you want Andrew to come looking for me..."

"No," she agreed quickly. "I don't want that." Then, "Chris... what do you watch *for*?"

He laughed. He thought in that moment of simple, easy laughter, of just feeling *good* for no specific reason, that he understood what was special about Lanie. He took her face between his hands and looked into her eyes and saw his smile reflected there and he thought, *This is good. This is important. This is worth holding on to.*

He said, "You know something? I think you just might be the most fun I've ever had, too."

FOR THE NEXT TWO DAYS Lanie lived the fairy tale, and it was more than she could have asked for. The sun-drenched days, the gently rolling sea, the snap of a white sail against blue, blue sky and sunsets so beautiful they made her eyes hurt. Deep rich nights that were never long enough, each a new adventure into passion... And Chris. Sometimes she wondered if he would have been so perfect—if any of it would have been so magically, flawlessly right—if they had not both known it would all have to end in only two days.

She stood on the deck on the night before they were to make landfall. The sky was a riot of stars, gemstones scattered over velvet, so vast and deeply dimensional that looking at it made her feel small and reverent. She could see the Big Dipper, the outline of Diana's Bow and part of the Bear. And Venus, her own personal wishing star.

Chris slipped his arms around her from behind, drawing her back against him. "Pirates, whales and other ships," he said.

She leaned into the cradle of his body, tilting her head back against his shoulder to look up at his face. "What?"'

"You asked me what we watched for."

"Ha. You forget I've been with you on those so-called watches and I know they're just an excuse to drink coffee and read dirty books."

He grinned into her hair. "I never read dirty books when you're around. That would be impolite."

Lanie smiled, but she felt a stab of pathos—no, it was more than pathos. It was something so sweet and sad that it hurt, physically, like a blossoming wound just below her left breast. In only a matter of days the feel of his body had become as familiar to her as her own. Yet this might be the last time she would stand within its shelter. Tonight would be the last time she would know the sensual mysteries only he could unfold for her and she felt as though she was only beginning to explore them. But she would never have enough of making love with him, of holding him, of simply standing with him like this, buffered against the wind, of looking at him, of hearing his voice. Three days was not enough, but it was all she had; she had known that from the beginning. And it was much, much more than she had ever expected.

Chris lifted his hand and pushed Lanie's hair away from her neck, lowering his head to place a kiss there. "What are you watching, pretty lady?"

She leaned her head against his shoulder again, looking up, and made one sweeping gesture across the sky. "That."

He followed her gaze across the bow, beyond the horizon and above. "What do you see there?"

She took a long, deep breath, sinking into him, swallowed by the sea and the vast, dizzying canopy of stars... and him. No, she would not be sorry. Not if she lived to be a hundred would she ever regret these last two days. No matter how much it hurt to know they were coming to an end.

"I see bears and huntresses and fallen heroes and fountains in the sky. I see worlds. Did you know some of the stars we're looking at now died before we were born? I see time. I see possibilities. Incredible, fantastical possibilities."

Chris's arms tightened around her waist. His voice was a little husky. "Have I told you today how glad I am I met you?"

A sudden thickness in Lanie's throat prevented her from replying, and she spent a moment fighting a wave of emotion she did not completely understand. Perhaps the hardest thing to deal with, the most impossible thing to comprehend, was Chris himself. He was rich, arrogant, spoiled and manipulative, accustomed to being in command and having his own way. These things she had known within half an hour of meeting him, but with her he was someone different.

He didn't have to be so wonderful. He didn't have to make her laugh at unexpected moments, wake her with coffee on a silver tray or surprise her with a scented bubble bath. He didn't have to turn and smile at her when she thought she was watching him unobserved, extend his hand to her when he stood alone at the wheel, share her silences and his own private times. He did not have to make her feel like a woman who was adored. She had never asked him for that and never expected it.

They had agreed to share a fantasy. He didn't have to make it seem so real.

And that, of course, was only going to make saying goodbye that much more painful.

The breeze seemed to carry a slight chill to it suddenly, and she shivered. Chris rubbed her bare arms with his hands, warming them. "Do you want to go below?"

She shook her head. "It's not a storm, is it?"

"No. We've been sailing north. The temperature always drops a few degrees along this latitude this time of year. I hope you brought a jacket."

"Sure I did. It's probably on its way to India by now."

Silence fell, and when she shivered again it wasn't entirely from the cold. He must have sensed her melancholy, even though she swore she would not spoil their last night together with sorrow or regret. And of course he knew the reason.

He nuzzled her cheek gently with his chin. "Penny for them."

"A bargain at twice the price."

"Come on, tell me a story."

She forced a smile. "Of sailing ships and sealing wax?"

"If that's what's making you feel so sad."

She gently released his arms from around her waist and stepped away. He let her go.

She walked to the rail. Her balance was as natural now as his was. "Do you know that poem about the tall ship and the star to steer her by?"

She could feel him watching her, and the effort it took for him not to close the few feet that separated them and touch her, hold her. She wished he would. Then she wouldn't have to say anything at all.

"Yes," he answered. "I know it."

She looked back at him, tried to smile and couldn't even meet his eyes. "I know it's corny, but it keeps running through my head. I guess I'll never hear it again without thinking of you."

He said, "There are worse things. Is that your sad story?"

So she straightened her shoulders, focused firmly on the far-distant sea and said, "Once upon a time there was a poor, but quite deserving princess..." But there she faltered, and had to swallow hard to get her voice back. She turned, bracing her hands against the rail, and her smile was soft and sad and genuine as she finished, "...who, for the very first time in her life got more than she deserved. Thank you for that, Chris. I'll never forget you, and I—I miss you already."

He took a step toward her, a hint of puzzlement in his smile. "Why do you have to miss me at all?"

For a moment Lanie didn't know what to say. "I thought—didn't you say we'd reach Player's Cay tomorrow?"

"That's the plan."

"Well then..." She floundered, confused. "I'll be going on board the *Rendezvous* and..." She looked at him with sudden question. "Unless you've changed your mind. Because it's perfectly okay if you have, I'll understand...."

"Good." He dropped his hands lightly on her shoulders. "Because I've changed my mind."

She stared at him wordlessly.

His thumbs caressed the gentle swoop of her collarbone, and his smile deepened. "Can you honestly tell me you'd prefer ten days on a luxury cruise ship with all the amenities of the finest hotels in Europe to being wet, cold and windblown here with me?"

Her heart stammered and skipped a beat. A part of her had been hoping he would ask, another part hardly dared to believe that he would. And yet another part was plunged into confusion, drowning her joy in uncertainty.

She searched his eyes. "I don't understand."

"What's there to understand?" He dropped a playful kiss on her nose. "I'm not finished with you yet."

But the smile in his eyes faded as he looked at her. "Wait a minute. Maybe I'm the one who's confused. You didn't really expect me to just let you go tomorrow, did you?"

Lanie fought her way through a tumult of emotion she had not expected and couldn't begin to sort out. Confusion, hope, delight, fear... Fear. It must have been that which directed her next words. She could think of no other explanation.

Her laugh was a little hollow as she repeated, "Let me go? I didn't realize I was your prisoner."

Frustration mixed with surprise flashed in his eyes. "You know what I mean."

"No, I don't." With a lift of her shoulders she stepped away from his touch. She meant the gesture, and the words, to be gentle; both seemed tinged with impatience. "I don't think you do, either."

He was frowning now. "I can't really believe that you expected me to just put you on that ship tomorrow. I can't believe that you'd want to go."

"I don't!"

He reached for her again. "Then what's the problem?"

She wanted to step into his arms, lose herself in his embrace, utter a mindless yes to whatever he said, whatever he wanted, because deep down it was only what she wanted too. And until she actually opened her mouth to speak she didn't have any idea what she was going to say.

"The problem is," she replied tightly, hugging her arms against a renewed chill, "that if I stay it will only be harder to say goodbye in ten days." She looked at him helplessly. "We both knew it was only for a little while. I was prepared to leave tomorrow. I don't want to, but I can. In another ten days . . . I'm not so sure."

But even as she spoke she saw the next ten days stretching out in an endless spiral of emptiness and longing, the luxurious surroundings of the *Rendezvous* wasted on her because once Chris was gone the adventure would be over. Or she could have ten more days of magic, ten more days of dreams come true...and at the end a parting so painful it would haunt her the rest of her life. How could she make a decision? Why was he making her choose?

She said, struggling to keep her voice even, "It's going to take a long time to get over you, Chris. Don't make it harder than it is."

"Maybe I don't want you to get over me."

The breath left her body, along with every thought and potential word. She simply stood there, hugging her arms tightly to her chest, and stared at him.

"Two days, two weeks—" he made a short frustrated gesture with his wrist "—who made these rules, Lanie? Who set the deadline, for God's sake? It's not over until we say it is. Maybe it doesn't have to be over at all, did you ever think of that? How can you know until you give it a chance?"

Her heart tumbled over in her chest and the stars actually seemed to shift their position in space as, just for a moment, she let herself think about it, she actually let herself imagine it could be possible, that he was serious, that it could be real.

But it was crazy, it was beyond imagining, and it hurt to think about just how far out of reach it was. "Chris, don't be ridiculous. You know that's not going to happen."

"How do you know?" he insisted. "Tell me just how you can be so sure."

"Because that wasn't the deal," she cried. "Because we both knew from the beginning it was just a game."

"Wait a minute." There was a note of real anger in his voice now. "You're saying I'm good enough to sleep with but not good enough to stay with?"

"You know that's not what I mean!"

"Then maybe you'd better be a little more specific because that's exactly what it sounds like to me."

Lanie drew a ragged breath and released it with a whisper. "God, I can't believe this." She pressed her fingers briefly to her lips, trying to stop the trembling, trying to marshal her thoughts. Five minutes ago life had been perfect and the night was full of magic; now it was dissolving around her like spun sugar in the rain, disappearing before her very eyes. The words Chris had said to her were ones any woman in her right mind would drop to her knees in gratitude for and they should have made Lanie the happiest person in the world. So how had it gone so wrong?

This was not how she wanted to spend her last night with him. This was not what she had expected at all.

"Chris, please, don't do this. If I could stay with you I would but—"

"But what? What have you got back in Iowa that's so important?"

"A *life!* A family—"

"A family who only wants to take advantage of you, a life that's so great you ran away from home and haven't given it a second thought since you left."

"That's not fair! You don't know anything about me or my life—"

His tone was cold, his expression remote as he replied, "Apparently not."

Lanie caught a breath that was very close to being a sob. She looked up at him, pleading, "Oh, Chris, I don't want to do this. Please, let's not fight. Everything was so perfect, don't let it end this way."

He stood less than two feet away from her. She wanted to close the distance, wrap her arms around him and bury her face in his chest, inhaling the scent and the feel and the taste of him, imprinting him on her memory forever. She wanted to wind back time and pretend the last few minutes had never happened. She wanted to go back to the fairy tale.

But she knew that was impossible when he said simply, "It doesn't have to end at all."

Lanie pressed her fingers to her temples, shaking her head adamantly against a sudden surge of anger for what he had taken from her. "You know it does! And the only reason you're doing this now is because it doesn't suit your convenience!"

"Damn it, you know that's not true—"

"It *is* true!" she cried. "Three days, two weeks, a month—you'd grow tired of me eventually and then we'd be right where we are tonight, only *you'd* be calling the shots. And that's what's really bothering you, isn't it? You're not finished with me yet. Well, maybe *I'm* finished with *you.*"

The minute she spoke she regretted the words. His expression was shrouded with shadows and difficult to read, but she could feel his surprise, his hurt, across the space that separated them. He said quietly, "I can't believe you mean that."

Lanie turned away miserably. "It doesn't matter. I—" she tried to look at him, but couldn't meet his eyes "—I'm sorry, Chris. Good night."

"Lanie." He caught her arm, forcing her to look at him. "What happened to the possibilities?"

It was a moment before she could answer, and then it was only with difficulty. "They were always," she replied tiredly, "just in my imagination." She pulled her arm away and left him.

Chris watched her go below, and when he was alone on the deck he clenched his hand into a tight fist and brought it down hard against the rail. "Damn!" he whispered. Nothing but the night answered.

He was angry—with her and with himself—but mostly he was incredulous. He couldn't believe what had just happened. He couldn't believe he was about to lose her and for no good reason at all. A mere four days ago he couldn't wait to be rid of her but the irony of it barely flickered across his mind. That was then and this was now, and it was too soon to let her go.

He knew why she was doing this and he knew she couldn't help it, but that did not make it any easier to deal with. She did not want to leave him now; he knew she didn't. But somehow he had to make *her* see that.

He wanted to follow her below, to lock the cabin door behind them and take her in his arms, drown her words with his kisses, replace her foolish arguments with passion, and he knew he could do it. For one more night he could make her believe in the magic, he could push the world aside...but he was very much afraid that in the morning it would make no difference. And worse, she might hate him for it. He couldn't go to her tonight. She was too hurt, confused and afraid. But she was also wrong.

All he needed was a chance to convince her of that.

After a time he went into the pilothouse and sat down at the map table. When Andrew came up to take his watch a few minutes later he found Chris finishing the last of his calculations.

Chris said without preamble, ''I figure we should make landfall about ten o'clock in the morning. We'll anchor on the north side of the island, which means we'll follow this course....''

Andrew listened attentively and studied the course Chris had charted. When he had finished he said, ''I understood the young lady was to join the party from the *Rendezvous.*''

"She was."

"Don't they disembark on the south side of the island?"

"That's right."

Andrew cleared his throat. "If we're on the north, won't that make it hard for her to make her connection?"

"I would say so, yes."

Andrew frowned a little. "I take it there's been a change of plans, then."

Chris smiled as he got to his feet. "That's right. Good night, Andrew."

Chapter Six

It serves you right, Lanie thought as she stood before the full-length mirror on the closet door.

She was wearing white culottes and a peach tank top, not her most flattering outfit but the only one she had left from her carry-on bag. Her eyes were puffy and shadowed from lack of sleep and she felt as miserable as she looked.

She had taken the chance of a lifetime and had managed to shred it to dust. She had stumbled into a miracle and, not content to let it play itself out, trampled the life out of it before it even had a chance.

All night long she had replayed the scene in her head and she still couldn't figure out how it had happened. *Chris had asked her to stay.* It was all she could ask for and she had not only turned him down, she had picked a fight with him over it. And in the process had lost not only two more weeks in paradise, but her last night of heaven.

And it was no one's fault but her own.

She gave the reflection in the mirror one last sour look. "Besides that," she muttered, "you're fat."

She moved briskly around the room, gathering up her things, repacking her tote bag, trying as much as possible to leave the cabin the way it had been when she found it...except that it would never be the same, not in her memory and not, perhaps, in reality. She liked to think that the stateroom would hold some trace of her when she was gone, something that Chris would find after she was gone, that would make him think of her. Because she would be thinking of him every single minute of every day for a long, long time.

It was late when she left the cabin, in part because she was reluctant to face Chris and in part because she simply did not want to leave. She didn't know how to say goodbye to him. Except for a few sobs muffled under the spray of the shower last night—tears that were as much from anger as regret—she had managed not to cry. But she wasn't sure how much longer she could keep the tears at bay when she saw him again, when she knew it was really goodbye. But even worse, she was afraid he wouldn't say goodbye. That he would have Joel or Andrew put her ashore and he wouldn't even give her a chance to tell him...

But she didn't know what she wanted to tell him. Perhaps that was what frightened her most of all.

The first thing she saw when she came on deck was the green of the island; after four days of nothing but sea and sky it was something of a shock. They were close enough that she could distinguish individual trees, but were nowhere near a beaching point. For some reason she had expected to just be able to step off the boat onto dry land; she realized now how silly that was. A boat the size of the *Serendipity* would not be able to dock near shallow water without the risk of running aground.

She did not see Chris.

She didn't see Joel either, or Andrew, and she was disappointed. She wanted to say goodbye to them and thank them for all they'd done. But they both knew she was leaving, and she could hear them going about their duties in the forward part of the boat. She thought they might be avoiding her and that made her feel desolate.

The morning air was cool on her bare arms, so she set her overnight bag on the deck and found a place in the sun to sit down and wait. She didn't see the *Rendezvous*, but Chris hadn't told her what time it was supposed to arrive. She wondered if there was any way she could get back to civilization without the luxury liner. She could no longer enjoy Chris's generosity, and the last thing she was in the mood for was a ten-day party.

"Hi."

At the sound of his voice her heart caught in her throat and she steeled herself to turn around, her smile already in place.

He was wearing white deck pants that ended just below his calves, a navy windbreaker over a T-shirt and, for the first time since she had known him, shoes. His face was somber, his eyes the color of the pre-dawn sea. Looking at him made her chest hurt.

He carried another jacket in his hand, white poplin, and he handed it to her.

She hesitated before accepting. "No, I—" But then she broke off and dropped her eyes. "Thank you." She pulled the jacket over her arms. Then, quickly before the threat of tears robbed her of her voice entirely, "Chris, I wanted to tell you—"

"Listen, about last night—"

They both broke off and with a faint shared smile acknowledged that there was really no need for words between them. Again Lanie felt that stab of loss and sorrow deep in her stomach. She had to tighten her muscles against it before she could speak.

"I said some stupid, ugly things," she said quietly. "I didn't mean them. I was just upset, and—scared."

"I guess I was a little heavy-handed," he admitted. "I'm sorry."

She looked up at him. She tried not to think about never seeing him again, about saying goodbye in a few minutes or a few hours and spending the rest of her life with nothing but memories and speculation about what might have been. She tried not to wish too hard.

"Lanie, I don't want it to end like this. Can't we talk about it?"

She swallowed hard and had to look away, over the gently lapping ocean waves to the green land beyond. "I don't know what to say."

He reached down and took both of her hands in his, drawing her to her feet. "I asked Joel to pack a picnic for us. I thought we could go ashore, if you want, and spend the afternoon together."

She thought, *Thank you, God.*

But she felt she had to say, "The *Rendezvous* . . ."

"Won't be leaving until late this afternoon. You have plenty of time."

She smiled. He really *was* more than she deserved. "A picnic sounds great, Chris. I'd love to."

She was amused to see that the small tender was already in the water and loaded with blankets and an insulated picnic bag. Of course it wouldn't occur to Chris that she might say no. And though she still believed in clean breaks, though she knew the time spent with him now would only make their eventual parting more painful, she would not have missed these last hours with him. Not at any cost.

THEY TIED OFF the tender on the beach and walked a few hundreds yards down a sun-dappled path through the tropical foliage, emerging on a small knoll with a panoramic view of the ocean. They spread the blankets over the sand, one to sit on and one to hold the food. Lanie laughed when she saw how much food Joel had packed, and Chris groaned. "I thought that bag was too heavy for an ordinary picnic. He must have thought we were catering a party."

There was a thermos of coffee, a bottle of wine, and several bottles of mineral water— "Just in case we can't decide what we want to drink," Lanie suggested as she set them out. Next she unpacked several different cheeses, still sealed in wax, a loaf of hard bread, a whole smoked chicken and what appeared to be the entire boat's store of fresh fruit.

"He must have been clearing out the storage space to make room for fresh provisions," Chris said, amused.

"Well, he obviously expected us to do nothing but eat."

"Could be." There was a twinkle in Chris's eyes as he reached for an apple. "He has a big crush on you, you know. Maybe this is his way of making sure he keeps you to himself."

Lanie blushed, surprised. "He does not. That's ridiculous."

"What's so ridiculous about it? It would be hard not to have a crush on you, and I speak from experience."

Lanie's heart picked up a quick pattering rhythm, and she smiled as she met his eyes. "Well, I'm afraid if Joel was trying to win my heart through my stomach his efforts have failed. You have nothing to fear from the competition."

But his expression was serious as he replied, "I'm not so sure about that. First I have to find out what my competition is."

Lanie avoided his eyes, busying herself with filling the plates.

Lanie took off her jacket while they ate, and Chris watched her arms and shoulders pinken with the sun. He knew he should tell her to put it back on but couldn't bring himself to: the way the tank top hugged her breasts and shaped her waist was entrancing. He didn't think she was wearing a bra, and it would be very unlike Lanie not to. He wondered if he would have a chance to find out today.

He wondered too what it was about her that he found so hard to turn away from, so impossible to put out of his mind, and he couldn't think of just one thing—he could think of dozens. Maybe it was the newness, the freshness of her. He wondered if in two weeks, or two months, his fascination with her would have waned; he had certainly lost interest in other women more quickly than that. And he wondered— however briefly—if part of it might be what Lanie had said last night, that he was only holding on to her because he did not like to have his plans thwarted. He wondered how he was going to make her see that what was between them—or what might be between them—was much more important than that.

He never once wondered whether he had done the right thing in bringing her here.

"Do you have any sunscreen in that portable trunk of yours?" he asked finally.

She turned from repacking the picnic bag and made a face at him. "If you're referring to my purse..."

"I am. And don't pack all that stuff away. We might want some more later."

"You've got to be kidding."

"The more we eat, the less we have to carry."

"You've got a point." After a few moments' rummaging in her purse she came up with a bottle of sunscreen and tossed it to him. "But there's no point in letting all this food spoil in the sun." She turned to finish rewrapping the cheese. "Besides, shouldn't we be getting back pretty soon?"

"There's no hurry."

Chris poured sunscreen in his hands, rubbed them together, and gently smoothed his palms over the semicircle of Lanie's back and neck that was exposed. He could feel her surprised tension at his touch and then the way that tension flowed away, melting into his fingertips. Her response to his touch, so absolute and so unquestioned, made him feel strong, powerful.

From not touching to touching, from conversation to intimacy, from friends to lovers, their relationship was as simple, and as complex as that. He wished he could make her see that things were not always as black and white as she wanted them to be.

He refilled his palms with sunscreen and stroked the back of her arms, now circling, now lightly massaging. Lanie could feel her spine grow weak, and her skin begin to glow with a thousand open nerve receptors, each one aching for his touch. *How can I leave this?* she thought.

But she couldn't go on avoiding the issue, pretending she didn't have to, forever.

She twisted around to look at him, swallowing hard to clear her throat. "Chris, I was wondering, I mean, I hate to ask, and if it's going to be any trouble at all please tell me but—I was wondering if there's any way I could just go directly back to Miami. Without the *Rendezvous.*"

His hands stopped in mid-motion. She thought he would move away from her but he didn't. He held her arms, and he said quietly, "Why do you keep doing that?"

It was she who had to move away, miserably avoiding his gaze. "Because I'm depraved. Because I enjoy punishing myself. Early childhood trauma. I don't know. But aren't you glad you're getting rid of me? I might turn out to be a real psychopath."

He stopped her babble, which was only growing more and more desperate, by placing his hands on her waist and turning her, gently but firmly to face him fully. His expression was calm and patient, and looking at him made Lanie want to cry.

"Just let me understand this. Are you homesick? Is there something—someone—at home you haven't told me about? Some reason you need to get back there right away?"

She was shaking her head long before he finished speaking. *No reason,* she thought, *except to be safe from you....*

"No. It's not that. I can barely remember what home looks like." She dropped her eyes. "I don't want to remember. Oh, Chris, don't you see?" She looked up at him, searching his eyes, pleading with him to understand. "That's what frightens me. I walked out on the only life I've ever known because I wanted to do something daring, exciting, *fun* for once in my life, before I got too old. I wanted to make just one of my dreams come true for just a little while. But that's all it was, just a dream. And now..." She searched for the words. "Now I'm finding out that I like all this—" she made an all-encompassing gesture that included him "—better than real life, and that scares me because I know it can't last."

She expected an impatient reply or a brisk dismissal or even some small affectionate joke to gently nudge her out of a mood that she had never wanted to become so serious. She never expected him to reply, quietly and reasonably, "Why can't it?"

She stared at him. "What?"

"Why can't it last?"

It was she who felt the surge of frustration then mixed with a generous dose of hurt and overlaid by a peculiar, heart-wrenching moment of hope that only served to turn her emotions into a knot of confusion. She said shortly, "If you have to ask, you have your answer."

"Come on, Lanie, that doesn't make any sense."

"All right." She drew a deep breath and faced him squarely. "All right, let's talk about making sense. We've know each other for four days. We come from different parts of the country, different backgrounds, we have nothing in common and we never would have even met if I hadn't been stupid enough to get on the wrong boat. So tell me, what *is* there to last?"

It was with a great effort that Chris kept his voice even, his temper calm. Every word she spoke frustrated him more, mostly because he knew she didn't mean half of it, if any at all. "We have more in common than you realize," he said deliberately. "Neither one of us likes it very much when things don't go the way we planned them. And the only reason we're fighting now is because we had different plans for how this relationship would go."

Lanie's throat hurt; every muscle in her body hurt with the effort of keeping her emotions under control. She focused on the bright blue glint of the ocean and it hurt her eyes, but that was good; it kept her mind off the much bigger hurt that was growing inside her. "I don't know what you're talking about."

"It's simple." His voice was curt. "You planned on three days of sun and fun and sex—maybe because you thought that was all I was offering, maybe because you thought that was all you deserved."

Even though she was half-turned from him Chris saw her flinch, and he was sorry. But he went on ruthlessly. "Maybe because you thought that's the way the game was played by the sophisticated jet set and you convinced yourself you could accept those rules. Well, you were wrong on all counts."

"Don't do this. There's no point in doing this...."

Chris didn't want to make her cry. Given a choice he would much rather be stretching her out on the blanket beneath him right now, tasting her sun-warmed flesh, watching her face grow soft with pleasure as she welcomed him to her. But some things were worth fighting for and he continued. "And if you think I was only interested in you for the short term—that I would have made love to you and planned to dump you in three days—then maybe you should just go and catch your ship back to Miami because it's obvious we don't know each other at all."

She turned a wide incredulous gaze on him. "Don't hold your ethics up for inspection to me, Chris Vandermere! Aren't you the same man who bribed me to stay aboard just so you wouldn't have to spoil your vacation plans? And you'll pardon me for saying so but I didn't notice you putting up much of a fight over *your* role in the fantasy! You were as happy as any man to have a bed partner for three days, a week, or until you got tired of me. It seems perfectly clear to me—"

"There you go again, making assumptions about me!" And even though Chris had vowed he wasn't going to let this get out of control, he seemed powerless to stop the anger from sharpening his voice, tensing the muscles of his jaw. Perhaps it was because he was beginning to realize he might lose this argument and that was a possibility that simply hadn't occurred to him before. "Who the hell do you think I *am* anyway? Some kind of TV playboy with scripted lines and plastic morals? Don't I get any credit at all?"

"I don't *know* who you are, any more than you know who I am! That's the whole point, that's what you keep trying to ignore—"

"Damn it, Lanie, why are you trying to make this so hard?" His voice was tight with frustration and barely controlled anger. "Why can't you just let it go?"

"Because it's my life!" Her eyes blazed, drying the film of tears. "Because to you it's just a game—the dashing pirate, prince of the seas, and his captured maiden—and you call the shots, you can start it or stop it at will, but I have a *life,* don't you understand that? I'm not a toy and I'm tired of playing!"

"I never treated you like a toy." He made no effort to disguise his anger now. His eyes were dark with it, his voice as cold as ice. "This is not a game to me."

Lanie caught a breath sharply, far back in her throat. She massaged the pain that choked her voice with her fingers. "Maybe that's the problem," she said quietly, after a time. "Maybe there's too much of the pirate in you, Chris—adventure on the high seas, plundering the boardroom, ravaging maidens..." She couldn't quite manage the smile she had intended. "You were born to it, but I'm just a small-town girl. What seems like a game to me is a way of life to you."

"I see." He was silent for a time, and Lanie could not make herself look at him. "And I suppose you're going to pretend you haven't enjoyed being part of that life."

She cast a quick, startled look at him, sharp with hurt. "That's not the point and you know it."

"Isn't it? For God's sake, what do you want from me, Lanie?"

For the longest time Lanie couldn't even think of the words to reply. How could any man be so impossible, so single-minded, so completely oblivious to any options other than his own? Chris made the rules, Chris called the shots, Chris decided when and where and how…and weren't those the very things she found so maddeningly, irresistibly attractive about him?

At last she didn't know anything else to say except, "What do you want from *me?*"

And he replied simply, immediately, "I want you to stay."

Lanie just stared at him, for what seemed like a very long time. Then she said simply, "How long?"

When a flicker of a question shadowed his eyes she repeated, "How long? Another week, a month? A year? I'll have to let my brother know, because he'll need to find someone else to keep his books until I get back. And in the meantime what am I suppose to do for a job? Or maybe I won't need a job at all, maybe we'll just be world travelers living on love and expectations because in fairy tales no one has to work for a living, do they? And after a month or a year, then what? Will you marry me?"

Chris could not remember ever having worked so hard to gain so little and the frustration that churned inside him was surely out of proportion to what was at stake. Why was she making this so complicated? Why had it become so desperately important to him that she agree with him, that he not lose her? She was right; they had known each other for only three days and he had said goodbye to many a woman on longer acquaintance with barely a backward glance. What was so special about Lanie? Why couldn't he just let her go?

But he didn't know; he only knew she *was* special. And she did not want to go, any more than he wanted to let her. Why couldn't she see that?

"For God's sake, Lanie, I'm not asking you to come live on my home planet with me, just stay in Miami for a while. I have a meeting in Los Angeles on the fifteenth I can't get out of, but after that there's nothing I can't clear from my schedule, no reason we can't take as much time as we want and spend it together, doing whatever we want. Why are you working so hard to make this impossible?"

"It might as *well* be your home planet," she returned helplessly, "because the worlds we come from are that far apart!"

She thrust her hands into her hair, drawing a tense breath, refusing to look at him. "Oh Chris, don't you see this is *exactly* what I'm talking about? For you anything is possible but for me it's not! You sit up in your big glass-walled office and control destinies via long distance, shuffle around millions of dollars in your spare time and then for fun you come out here and play pirate for a week or two—but always, of course, within arm's reach of the imported beer and never more than a radio call away from help if you should get into trouble—you don't have a *clue* about real life!"

And that was enough. Chris said shortly, "And you do? Locked away in Nowhere, Iowa, playing indentured servant to your brother and sister because you're too afraid to take a chance on having a life of your own? *That's* real life?"

"That's not fair!"

Chris caught her arms, turning her around on the sand, forcing her to look at him. "Damn it, Lanie, what do you expect? Do you want me to say I love you? You wouldn't believe me if I did and you won't give me a chance to even find out it's true. Do you want me to promise you forever? Will you do the same for me? You're worth fighting for and I'm doing the best I can but you've got to tell me what you *want.*"

Lanie's heart was pounding, twisting in her chest. His hands were hard on her arms and there was fire in his eyes and she wanted to jerk away and run from him, she wanted to burst into tears, she wanted to sink into his arms. She did none of those things. She caught her breath, and the emotion that spread through her was too complex, too strange to even define. He had said she was worth fighting for. He thought there was a chance for them. She knew it was impossible, but oh, she wanted to believe, she wanted to pretend, she wanted it to last just a little longer....

"I don't want to leave you."

The words were hers. The voice, soft and subdued, was hers. But even as she heard the words she could not believe it was she who had spoken…and then she was glad. Because it was true, it was what she had wanted from the beginning and what she had been trying to fight all day. She simply wanted to stay with him.

The moment seemed suspended forever. She felt Chris's slow inhalation of breath, the slight tightening pressure of his fingers on her arms. There was a moment of heart-stabbing alarm when she thought that after all this he might now reject her, that she had gone too far.

Then he said huskily, "I know." And covered her mouth with his.

His heat, his taste spread through her like molten lava, taking her strength and her reason and drawing them into him. He kissed her and she was mindless. He touched her and all of her carefully fortified defenses melted like wax in the sun. It seemed a perfectly reasonable trade to Lanie: the world for another moment in his arms.

Chris's hand slipped beneath the hem of her culottes, caressing her knee, closing with a firm possessive strength on the flesh of her thigh. She knew that they would end this day by making love here on the beach and dizziness soared inside her head. He wanted her to stay and she wanted it to last even if it was only for a few more days. More memories, more dreams, and when it was over . . .

It would be enough. She was sure it would be.

His breath fanned across her cheeks as he lifted his face, and her fingers pressed against the back of his neck, urging him back to her. But he reached up and took her hand, drawing it down to his chest, over his heart. The gentle blur of his smile went through her, heating from the inside like the slow radiance of an unseen sun.

"See what you do to me?" He held her fingers against the strong, fast beating of his heart for a moment, then moved her hand downward, below his waist. "And this . . ."

She felt his heat and hardness, caressing his shape through the cotton fabric, watching the light that played in his eyes in response to her touch. Knowing his pleasure was a pleasure in itself. How could she have thought of leaving him, now or ever? How could she have wanted to?

Chris dropped a kiss onto her neck as she let her hands drift downward, caressing his thighs, then up again, spreading over his back. She felt his chest expand with a breath, long and slow. For a moment they simply held each other.

Then Chris threaded his fingers through her hair, tilting her face upward to receive the gentle touch of his lips. He smiled softly into her eyes. "I'm glad you changed your mind."

"I'm glad you won another argument."

His smile deepened and his hand moved beneath her left breast, thumb and forefinger braced beneath its weight for a moment, the heel of his hand pressed over her heart. Her pulse sped. "I don't always win, you know."

"Just when it counts?"

His fingertip circled her nipple, a light, teasing tantalizing motion that promised more than it delivered. She was not wearing a bra and the aching peak stiffened in immediate response to his touch. He watched her, his eyes reflecting pleasure in her reaction, as he answered, "Right. And this counted. A lot."

The thrill that went through her wasn't entirely due to the sensation he was creating with his fingertips. Yet it was a moment before she could find the breath to reply, "If you had asked me to stay again this morning, we wouldn't have had to argue at all."

His eyes crinkled at the corners and his clever, skillful fingers left her breast to tease the curve of her collarbone. "My fault. I should have known."

Lanie leaned into him, draping her arms around his neck, tasting the heated, textured flesh of his throat. She felt a surge of power in his soft sound of pleasure, in the fingers that tightened on her leg. She murmured, teasing him a little, "Do you think we should radio the captain of the *Rendezvous,* or something, and tell him I won't be coming aboard?''

Chris threaded his fingers through her hair, tilting her head back. Deliberately he placed a kiss on one eyelid, then the other, closing them.

"I already did," he said.

Chapter Seven

The minute Chris spoke he knew he'd made a mistake, but he wouldn't have been able to say at that moment whether the biggest mistake had been in deceiving her or admitting to the deception. Until that very moment, until she looked at him with those big, stunned brown eyes, he had not even thought of what he had done in terms of deception.

He felt her stiffen in his arms. "You did what?"

And the worst was he didn't know what to say to her. He had never had to explain himself to anyone before and the necessity for doing so now left him frustrated and at a loss, and with the beginnings of what he thought was a very justifiable anger.

Oh, he knew why he had done it, and given the choice he would not have acted any differently. He hadn't wanted to lose her, and calling off the *Rendezvous* was the most graphic way he knew of demonstrating that. She would call that selfish. He had also known that she would change her mind and he had been right; she would call that manipulative and patronizing. He wanted to give them a chance to find out just how far their relationship could take them, for her sake as well as his own, and there was nothing wrong with that. But when she looked at him she made him feel like a criminal and there was something *very* wrong with that.

Lanie pushed slowly away from him and got to her feet. She looked down at him for a moment with a mixture of weariness and contempt. "Well," she said, "I walked right into that one, didn't I?"

She turned to scoop up her purse and stalked away.

"Damn!" Chris ground out fiercely.

He thought about not following her—not until he got his own mixed emotions under control at any rate. But in the state she was in who could guess what she would do when she reached the tender? After another moment and another oath he grabbed the picnic bag and the blankets and went after her.

He caught up with her midway down the path. She spoke without looking back, her voice low with anger and breathless with exertion. "You can take me back to Miami or you can call another boat or you can drop me at the nearest island with an airstrip or a telephone. Or you can leave me here and I'll wait for the next ship."

He caught a branch that she had pushed carelessly aside before it slapped him across the face. "All right," he said shortly, "you win. We have nothing in common. We come from different worlds and our priorities are poles apart. I don't understand you. But would you mind telling me exactly which one of your midwestern values I've offended this time?"

She stopped and whirled on him, her eyes blazing. "The one that doesn't like to be lied to, or used or manipulated! The one that would like to be treated with a little more respect than—than just a game piece that you can move around and rearrange to amuse yourself!"

"Did I hear you say something about *using* someone? Aren't we dealing with a double standard here?"

Her face was flushed and her eyes were shiny; Chris couldn't be entirely sure whether the brilliance was from anger or tears and at that point wasn't greatly interested in finding out.

"You could have *asked* me!" she cried.

"I *did* ask you!"

Lanie turned and marched down the path again.

Chris stood there for a moment longer, wrestling with his own fury and defeat. He had never been reduced to chasing after a woman before, figuratively or literally. Since last night she had put him through more emotional cartwheels than anyone had before in his life, and he had let her. He had even believed—he had tried every method at his disposal to make *her* believe—that there was something special between them, something that, if given a chance to grow could make any sacrifice worth it.

But as clear and urgent as all of that had been only a few minutes ago, it was now just as clear that he had been wrong. He had lost and he hated losing but it was time to admit his mistake. He didn't have the skill or the time or the energy to fight his way through all the layers of her insecurity, and trying to do so was only making him crazy. Why had he ever thought he wanted to?

She was right. He had gotten carried away with the fantasy, looking so hard to find something he hadn't even, until this moment, realized he wanted that he had imagined possibilities where none existed. He had behaved like a hormone-driven adolescent since the moment he had met her and only now was he coming to his senses. There were hundreds of women in the world, thousands, and not one of them was worth this turmoil.

If she expected him to plead with her to stay this time she would be very surprised. He would radio for a helicopter pickup tonight—maybe one for each of them. His vacation was already ruined, and he had important things to deal with back in the real world.

He let her get quite a bit ahead of him, and when he emerged from the foliage she was standing on the small beach near the surf, her arms folded over her chest, her mouth tight with anger—or perhaps hurt. Again, he couldn't tell, and again he didn't want to.

"Very funny, captain," she said. "I suppose this was all part of your master plan, too."

Chris dropped the blankets and the picnic bag on the sand and started toward the tender. "Believe me, lady, the last thing I have right now is a sense of humor. I don't have a master plan, either, unless it's to get you back to the boat and out of my life."

Her lips curved into a bitter, humorless smile. "And just exactly how are you planning to do that without a tender?"

Chris had reached the edge of the surf and there he stopped, staring at the place the tender was supposed to be. He had been so certain that it *was* still there, right where he had left it, that it wasn't until he was almost upon the place where it should have been did he actually realize it was gone. The sturdy piece of driftwood to which it had been tied was still there, and he could even see the indentation just above the tide line where the bow had rested. But the little boat was not there.

Chris had never tied a shoddy knot in his life; nonetheless the first thing he did was turn to scan the water for signs of a bobbing boat come loose from it mooring. He froze, staring. "It's gone."

"No kidding, Sherlock! So what was the theory—
that no woman could resist a night stranded on a desert island with you?" Lanie's voice was shaking with
anger and humiliation. "Is there no end to your ar-
rogance? For God's sake—"

"The *Serendipity*. It's gone."

LANIE FOLLOWED his gaze over the empty sea, but it
took her a long time to comprehend the significance
of what he was saying. When she did she took a long
deep breath and said slowly, "You are beyond be-
lief."

She thrust both hands through her wind-tossed hair,
and the words she wanted to fling at him tumbled over
each other so fast they got tangled up in her throat and
she couldn't even speak. She was angry, yes, at his
high-handed assumptions and disregard for her needs,
but there was an even deeper anger because she had
believed in him, because she had let her better judg-
ment go and she had trusted him only to find there was
nothing sincere about him at all.

"Very good," she said, with amazing calm. "Blankets, picnic basket, wine...a beautiful, heart-
wrenching speech asking me to stay. But it didn't
matter what I said because the *Rendezvous* is already
gone and just to make certain I couldn't change my
mind, so is the *Serendipity* and the tender! For God's
sake, Chris, do you this for a *profession?* Do you sit

around in your spare time thinking up new and out-
rageous ways to seduce women? And why even
bother? I mean, talk about overkill! All you had to do
was look at me to seduce me. Did you really think that
a night spent sleeping on the sand with the fleas and
the mosquitoes was going to make you any more ir-
resistible? But wait!''

She snapped her fingers as though in sudden inspi-
ration. Her voice was growing shrill as her hurt and
disappointment turned to sarcasm. ''What do you
want to bet that somewhere back in the jungle there is
a clearing with a candlelit table set for two and a tent
all decked out with mosquito netting and cushions like
something out of *Lawrence of Arabia?* What, did I say
cushions? Why not a waterbed? Chris Vandermere
never does anything halfway!''

''Shut up.''

Lanie had turned back toward the jungle as though
to look for the mythological clearing, but the harsh
words, the dull, unimpassioned way in which he spoke
them stopped her short. She turned back slowly to
look at him. ''*What* did you say?''

He stood with the surf lapping at his deck shoes,
staring at the horizon line with an expression so tight
and grim that, had Lanie noticed it earlier, it would
have left her no breath for the vitriol she had just
hurled at him.

Without looking at her and still in that distant, dismissive tone, he said, "If you go back into the jungle you'd better plan on finding your way out by yourself because I'm not coming after you."

Lanie felt as though she had been punched in the stomach. The shock and the hurt literally took her breath away, and for a long time she couldn't even think.

She watched in stunned silence as Chris's hands balled into fists and he said, very lowly, with terrifying clarity, "Son of a bitch. They really did it. They stole my boat."

It wasn't until he actually spoke the words that he believed the evidence of his eyes. The *Serendipity* was gone. The sense of outrage and betrayal that streaked through him was the same as that of any captain who had ever been faced with a mutinous crew. He had made his orders very clear: The *Serendipity* was to stay at anchor, safely offshore, until he returned. There were a couple of acceptable, though highly unlikely explanations for why she was gone, but there was no reason why the tender was also missing.

And that was when he had to face the unavoidable conclusion: the *Serendipity* had been stolen. He had been stranded so that Andrew and Joel could make off with his yacht. Fury and self-loathing swept through him and he swore viciously, turning sharply away from the panorama of empty sea.

What an idiot he had been. Was there anything more foolish, more *worthless* than a sailor who would let his boat be stolen right out from under him? What, he wondered bitterly, would Grandpa Hannibal think of *that?*

What had he been thinking of, to let Personnel assign a crew to his personal yacht? Sailors weren't picked like grocery clerks or short-order cooks; he couldn't have taken half a day to choose the men to whom he would be entrusting his boat, not to mention his life, for two weeks. And that was another thing: the *Serendipity* didn't require a three-man crew; he should have become suspicious when he realized two of them had been assigned. Because it would take two of them to get the boat to port now.

He repeated that single harsh, vulgar oath again, and then determinedly tried to wrestle down his temper. He wanted to hit something, kick something, *kill* something, but there was nothing within reach but sand and surf and neither would make very good targets. So he took slow deep breaths and focused on clearing the red haze from his mind so he could think of what to do.

The *Rendezvous* was probably still within radio range, and though he would not expect them to bring that big ship back to pick him up, that was his best bet for getting a priority chopper out here—and for reporting the theft. Unfortunately, the nearest radio was on the other side of the island.

Damn, he had made it easy for them. They must have fallen out of their bunks laughing over how easy it was going to be. Rich young playboy, too busy—or too stupid or too lazy—to hire his own crew, too wrapped up in his own pleasure to pay attention to what was going on around him, making his elaborate plans for seduction and playing right into their hands. He could hardly have been more cooperative if he had handed them the deed to the boat gratis.

"Chris?" It was Lanie's voice, small and uncertain. "Are you serious?"

Chris had not forgotten her, but for the space of these last few horrible minutes she had been far, far in the back of his mind. He looked at her now and the sight of her only reminded him of his own stupidity and failure. He knew it wasn't her fault but he wanted to blame her.

Bitterness was sharp in his voice as he returned, "Of course I'm not serious. I'm never serious about anything, am I? Why should I pick now to start? I just thought this would be the perfect way to cap off a great day of sun and surf—wouldn't it be fun to be stranded on an island with a woman who just told me to go to hell while two men I don't know sail away with my yacht? Hell, yes, I'm serious! Do I look like I'm hiding a boat up my sleeve?"

It took a while for Lanie's head to stop spinning long enough for her to realize he was, indeed, serious. He hadn't planned this—or if he had, something had gone terribly, terribly wrong. "There—there must be some mistake."

He turned a look on her that was scathing enough to draw blood. "I'm aware that you don't have much faith in my ability to get along in what you call the real world, but I've got to tell you, lady, it would be hard for even me to make a mistake about something like this."

She shook her head, hard. "No, I mean Joel and Andrew wouldn't steal your boat! You're wrong, why would they want to—"

"Why would two out-of-work sailors want to steal a yacht worth almost a hundred-grand? Why, gee, Lanie, I can't think of a single reason. Maybe they want to strip it and sell it for parts!"

"I can't believe they would—"

"It doesn't matter much what you believe, does it? It's done!"

"How are we going to get home?"

His eyes blazed with contempt and impatience. "Well, that would be the question of the hour, wouldn't it?"

He drew a sharp breath and looked as though he would have said more but then changed his mind. He said only, shortly, "Stay here."

He pushed past her and started walking down the beach. He didn't even glance back in her direction.

Lanie watched him until his figure was a small silhouette far down on the beach, and then the curve of the land hid him from view. She wondered where he was going, what his plan was, if he intended to come back at all. She wondered how something so wonderful had started to come apart at the seams so quickly. She stood there alone on an empty beach and fought back the urge to cry.

She should have been laughing. She had wanted adventure, hadn't she? Wasn't this poetic justice? In four short days she had managed to find and lose the man of her dreams, sail away on a luxury yacht and get dumped on an uninhabited island without so much as a change of underwear, lost her luggage *twice*... For any other woman, being stranded on a deserted island with a man like Chris would be a dream come true. For Lanie it should have been a dream come true, but no. She had to make sure he hated her before he got stranded with her. How could they spend the night together when they had both made it clear that another hour in each other's company was more than they were willing to take?

And it was becoming apparent that they were going to have to spend the night, or at least a portion of it, unless Chris had gone in search of a telephone or another boat. The sun was sinking low on the horizon and doing it quickly, as it did this time of year, taking with it some of the warmth of the day. Lanie shivered in the breeze and reached for her jacket—Chris's jacket.

The light on the water turned from gold to silver and then faded altogether, leaving black and indigo streaks across the horizon. She spread out a blanket and sat on it, drawing up her legs and wrapping her arms around them to keep warm, watching for Chris. Where had he gone? How long would he be gone? Her nerves were almost at the snapping point when she saw him appear, barely a shadow against the deepening twilight.

She stood up, trying to look casual as she brushed nonexistent sand off her culottes, deliberately restraining herself from running to him. She could tell he was carrying something and she had vague notions about a radio or an inflatable life raft or even an insulated sleeping bag. When he drew close enough for her to see what was in his arms, disappointment and anxiety drew her nerves taut again.

"That's *it?*" she said incredulously. "You've been gone all this time and all you come back with are some broken pieces of wood?"

"I was lucky to find this," he said. "We're going to need a fire." Wordlessly he knelt on the ground and stacked the wood for burning.

"To signal someone?" She was thinking of planes or helicopters or even ships at sea.

He didn't look up. "To keep warm."

Those simple words seemed to signify the end of hope—for that night at least. A man who was expecting to be rescued could put up with some slightly uncomfortable temperatures for a few hours. The shiver that went through her was more from dread than the chill that had crept into the sea breeze.

"I didn't know you smoked," she said.

"I don't."

"You just carry matches for the fun of it?"

She saw the muscles of his jaw tighten and his hand hesitate over the firewood and until that moment she really hadn't even asked herself whether she was honestly trying to be helpful or just trying to make him feel foolish—as foolish as she had felt sitting on the sand all that time wondering if he was coming back for her. But it didn't matter what her intentions had been; what she had done was only too obvious.

She picked up her purse, rummaged through it for a few minutes and came up with a book of matches. She tossed them to him.

"I collect them," she explained with an uncomfortable shrug. "Restaurants, hotels, souvenirs of my vast and colorful travel experience."

Chris glanced at the cover. It was from a place called Beef Man—Family Night Special: All You Can Eat

$4.95. Camden, Iowa. A million miles from here. A million miles from anything he had ever known.

He struck a match. The wind blew it out. He turned his back to the wind and tried again.

Lanie watched him go through half a book of matches and by that time it had become a battle of wills between him and the wind. He was losing.

Lanie returned to her purse, tore out an empty page from her address book and twisted it into a spiral. "Let me try." She snatched the matches from him.

The paper caught on the second try and she carefully shielded the tender flame with her free hand. "Quick, we need more paper. The napkins from lunch!"

Chris went to the picnic bag and returned in a moment with a handful of paper napkins, which he began to stuff beneath the firewood. Lanie held the burning paper spiral to the napkins until they caught and began to blaze, and by that time Chris was ready with some thin slivers of driftwood to use as kindling.

"Girl Scouts?" he asked dryly.

She shook her head, sitting back on her heels to observe the fire cautiously. "Trying to start a barbecue on a windy day."

Chris slanted her a peculiar look, but all he said was, "You do good work."

He arranged the burning kindling so that it would catch the other wood, and waited to make sure it did.

Then he picked up the matches she had dropped in the sand and offered them to her.

She shook her head quickly. "You keep them." Already she was beginning to feel as though she had committed some cardinal breach of protocol by coming between a man and his fire.

Chris slipped the matches into his pants pocket and went back for his jacket and a blanket. He laid it out on the sand with the picnic bag. "Dinner is served."

Lanie looked at the bag, but did not open it. "I guess now we know why he packed so much extra food."

But she still found it hard to believe. They had both been so nice, so professional, so... *nice*. But then she didn't suppose that anyone who applied for work aboard a hundred-thousand-dollar yacht would go around wearing a sign proclaiming I Am A Thief. And it seemed pretty certain now that they were *not* coming back.

She looked at Chris. The light was gone now, and the feeble glow of the firelight painted shadows across his face. It was still a handsome face, strong and noble and firm-featured, and it could still cause a little catch in her throat when she looked at him. But it was the face of a man so far distant from her now that she barely knew him at all. How could so much have changed in such a short time? How had this *happened?*

She endured the silence as long as she could, and then she drew a breath. "Don't you have something to tell me?"

He glanced up from the methodical job he was making of feeding small sticks into the fire. "Like what?"

She worked hard to keep her voice even. "Look, I know I'm only a mere woman and undoubtably the cause of all your troubles but you've got to admit I do have a vested interest in knowing what we're going to *do*."

Chris's attention was on the fire. "The company complex—storehouse, fuel tanks, caretaker's cottage and radio—is on the other side of the island. I suggest we try to get to it."

Lanie seized on two words with unmitigated relief. *Caretaker's cottage.* "Then we're *not* alone! The caretakers—they probably have boats. Who would live on an island without a boat? They probably take it out every day and in the morning they'll come sailing by and see us or take a walk on the beach ... Why are we building a fire when we could be walking over there right now?"

He was shaking his head long before she finished speaking and impatience had crept back into his tone. "In the first place, we can't just 'walk over there.' In the second, no one's going to be walking—or sailing—by here. There aren't any caretakers, and the cottage is just a place for the attendants to stay when the ships are calling."

"Attendants? You mean they don't live here?" Then a slowly unfolding sense of dread filled her. "What do you mean—*when* the ships are calling?"

Chris had walked almost two miles—hard, angry miles—before his mind was clear enough for the obvious to occur to him, and he hadn't liked discovering it then any more than he liked telling it to her now. "About once a season the ships' schedules lag so that nothing calls here for about three weeks. The attendants go home, the island is unstaffed."

It was, in a way, rather surprising that he even remembered that piece of information.

"The *Rendezvous* took the attendants back with it today. There won't be another ship by here until sometime next month."

Lanie felt her throat begin to close up with horror and disbelief and she still refused to accept what she was hearing. "You can't mean that. Maybe not any of your ships—cruise ships—but *something* has got to come by. Sailboats or fishing boats or— For God's sake, where *are* we?"

Still he did not look at her. His voice was even, but preoccupied. "It's a private island, out of the major traffic lanes, that's why we bought it. The chances of someone just stopping by are slim to nil."

Lanie took a slow, deep breath. "But you said there was a radio, right?"

"That's right."

"And they didn't take it with them? We can call somebody to come pick us up?"

Chris nodded.

"Well, how long will it take us to get to it? How big can this island be, anyway?"

"About ten miles long, maybe twice as wide."

Lanie tried to hide her dismay. She squared her shoulders and mentally revised her picture of a brief morning jaunt back to civilization.

"All right," she said. "Ten miles. A lot of people run ten miles on the beach every morning."

He cast her a glance that persuaded her to revise her statement. "All right, so maybe nobody runs ten miles every morning. But there's certainly no reason we can't walk ten miles in a day."

"Twenty," he corrected, and she stared at him. "We can't go around. We have to go across."

"Do you mean—through the jungle?"

Chris tossed the last small stick into the fire, dusted off his hands and got up. He picked up the second blanket and shook out the sand with a snap of his wrist. "It's not a jungle. It's a tropical forest."

"A tropical forest has wooden walkways and horticultural signs posted every few feet. *This* is a jungle. Besides, it's twice as far! Why can't we—"

"Because the beach doesn't go all the way around the island," Chris replied shortly. He spread out the blanket near the fire and sat down. "Most of the coastline is so rugged even a mountain climber couldn't get over it. There are only two ways to get from here to there—by boat, and straight across."

No. This has got to be some kind of joke, Lanie thought. Things like this just didn't happen in real life, not even to her. He had to be making this up. He *had* to be.

But one look at his closed, stone-hard face assured her that if this was a game, he was no more a willing participant than she was.

She thrust her fingers through her hair, grasping for composure and finding only the fraying ends of incipient panic. "This is just great," she muttered. "What did you need an island so *big* for?"

Chris merely said, "We should eat something and get some sleep. We'll have to start early in the morning."

It was an innocent comment, even sensible, but to Lanie it seemed like the last straw. The carefully pieced-together edges of her control snapped and she grabbed the strap of the picnic bag, drawing back her arm to hurl it at him.

In an instant he was beside her, staying her arm with a grip hard enough to bruise, his eyes blazing.

"Let me go!" she cried.

"You idiot! Those bottles are breakable!"

She tried to wrench her arm away, but he shook her. "The only fresh water on this island may well be in that bag," he told her lowly, breathing hard, "and if you think I'm going to die here because of your temper tantrum—"

"If anyone dies here it will be your fault, you know that, don't you? *Yours!*" Her voice was shrill and thick with venom, and though some dim faraway remnant of reason pleaded with her to be silent she couldn't. Fear and anger and hurt churned a poisonous potion inside her and she was as much a victim of its toxicity as was Chris. "Is this what you planned, Mr. Captain of Industry? The man who can turn back seven-hundred-ton ships and send people scurrying in a hundred different directions at once with a wave of his hand and who *always* gets what he wants—is this what you wanted? Is it? Because it's sure as hell what you've got!"

His grip on her arm was painful and the fire in his eyes briefly, shockingly intense but that was not what held Lanie paralyzed, held tight in the grip of the palpable fury that surged between them. It was her own knife-sharp, bitterly intense and painfully simple rancor. He had deceived her, he had brought her here and stranded her here, she was cold and frightened and miserable and it was all his fault and she hated him for it.

She could see the reflection of her own malicious acrimony in his eyes, and for a moment they were locked in silent combat, two strangers who once had looked at one another with nothing but tenderness and who were now willing to go to war over an insulated bag and a few bottles of mineral water. It was only a moment, but in that moment something essential between them died a swift and violent death.

Chris released her arm abruptly. His voice was cool with disdain, his expression opaque. "Let's not turn this into *Lord of the Flies* on the first night, okay?" He released her arm.

Her arm throbbed dully from the force of his grip, and she rubbed it absently. The aching hollowness that was spreading slowly outward from the pit of her stomach was big enough to swallow up any lesser pains. And though she knew she should apologize for her earlier outburst she couldn't. That was bad enough. But the worst part was she was not at all sure she would ever be able to forgive Chris... for what he had done, for what he had taken from her. For making her hate him.

She was still holding the handles of the picnic bag. She set it carefully on the ground. Chris followed the movement with his eyes and then, after a moment, got up and went back to his own blanket on the other side of the fire. Lanie watched as he wrapped himself in his blanket and lay down upon the sand. After a moment she did the same.

It was barely six o'clock, the sand was hard, the wind was cold and the surf was loud. Lanie was too miserable and worried to even think about sleeping, even if she had been tired. For the second night in a row she was sleeping alone when that was the last thing she had expected to be doing.

The silence went on forever. The fire began to die. Lanie had never felt so bleak and alone in all her life.

After a long, long time, she said, with an effort, "Chris. I'm sorry about your boat."

He was so long in replying that she thought he hadn't heard, or that he had fallen asleep. When at last he spoke his voice was tired and distant, and the emptiness behind the words went straight through her soul.

"I know," he said. He turned over on his side, his back to her. "Good night."

Lanie lay there shivering in the dark, wishing she knew what to say, or what to do, to turn back time and make everything all right between them again. But whatever had once been between them was gone now, and she did not know how to get it back. Perhaps that was because it had never really lived outside her imagination—and his.

She watched until the last hardy embers of the fire turned from red to orange to dull, dead gray. She watched the stars come out, one by one, and as hard as she looked she couldn't find one that looked familiar. Finally she watched as the stars were swallowed by the coming dawn, fading away like the memory of a dream. And still she lay wakeful, cold and alone.

Chapter Eight

Chris awoke after a few hours of fitful sleep with a sore throat and a headache. It was that flat gray hour just before dawn, cold and still. That time of day was no stranger to him, but never had it been so ugly, so completely devoid of possibilities. He had hoped things would look better in the morning; instead they couldn't have looked more grim.

He sat up, wincing as he did so. Every joint in his body was stiff, and bones he didn't even know he had ached with dampness and cold. Lanie was asleep so he moved carefully, not wanting to disturb her. She had been wakeful until an hour or so ago, and she would need all the rest she could get.

He got to his feet silently and stepped across the remnants of the fire, looking down at her for a moment. She was curled into a tight ball, her tousled hair sprinkled with sand and shielding her face. There were gaps where the blanket didn't completely cover her body; her fingers, her knees, and her toes were red with cold. Very carefully Chris draped his own blanket over her, and he felt a twisting ache in his chest as he stepped away. How could he be so tuned in to her that he could tell when she was awake without looking at her or touching her, but not know how to tell her he was sorry?

He could feel tension like steely fingers creep up the back of his neck, pressing against his throat. He strengthened his muscles against it and took a deep breath. He left Lanie to sleep and unzipped the picnic bag quietly. The coffee inside the thermos was stonecold, but he poured a cupful anyway and took it down to the shoreline.

He didn't have the faintest idea how they were going to get out of this.

He knew the general layout of the island only because he had glanced at the map when he was plotting the course that would bring the *Serendipity* around to the north side. He had sailed around the island and once he had hosted a party for some of the top executives and their wives at the pavilion, which was the only reason he knew—in general terms at least—where the complex was located.

He knew if they headed due south they should eventually emerge within a mile or two of the beach, and from there it would be possible to find the complex. He did know that it would be impossible to hold a straight course moving overland, and without a compass he wasn't even sure he could hold a generally southern course. He would have given half of all he owned at that moment for a map of the island.

Chris sipped the coffee. It tasted bitter and slimy but it did soothe his throat somewhat. He wondered if Lanie had any aspirin in her purse—which was a ridiculous thought. He wouldn't have been surprised if she pulled out an entire pharmacy from the depths of that canvas bag, like a magician drawing out a never-ending string of scarves from his sleeve. Chris only hoped that aspirin was the only medicine they would need before this was over.

Twenty miles of unfamiliar jungle between them and their only chance of rescue, no survival equipment or emergency supplies or even a compass; enough food and water for maybe three days... He wasn't prepared to deal with this. How could anyone have been prepared for this?

He could feel the tension again, gripping his spine. He fought it off.

He ran the largest privately-owned shipping concern in the country. He had been fighting his way through the corporate jungle for the past five years. Finding his way from one end of his own island to the other should barely present a challenge. He faced crises every day of his life. Masterful decisions were second nature to him. Survival was the name of the game and doing the impossible was just another requirement for the job. He could do this thing. He had to.

He supposed there was a part of him that had always wondered what it would have been like to live in the days of Hannibal, to test the limits of one's courage and ingenuity in real life. He supposed there was a part of him that wondered how well he'd fare in a real challenge of endurance, how well he'd live up to his swashbuckling image. "Well, skipper," he murmured out loud. "You've just gotten your chance."

IF A MAN COULD WALK 3.5 miles per hour, Lanie thought, and the island was as Chris speculated twenty miles across, and they walked eight hours a day... She did some careful calculations in her head and was greatly cheered by the results. There was no reason at all they shouldn't reach the other side of the island before nightfall—long before. And she could stand anything for one day.

So far it wasn't so bad. They had been moving for about an hour—3.5 miles, Lanie thought optimistically—and for most of the way the ground had been sandy, the foliage low and sparse. Only now were they beginning to move into taller jungle, with prickly undergrowth that left a network of fine scratches on her lower legs and a profusion of waist-high and taller trees that reminded her of walking through the houseplant section of the local nursery.

Chris was in the lead and it was difficult to keep up with him in her thin slippery sandals, but she didn't complain. For one thing, she wanted to move as quickly as possible, for the faster they walked the faster they could get out of here. For another, she did not want to do anything to disturb the cautious truce that seemed to have been established between them this morning.

She had wanted to. When he had slung the picnic bag over his shoulder and led the way into the jungle she had wanted to argue with him. She didn't want to try to cross the island; once they were in the interior they would be lost to all hope of rescue. But Chris had been so sure this was the right thing to do, and it was his island after all. She gave him credit for knowing enough about their options to make an informed decision, and so far it looked as though he had been right.

No sooner had she come to that conclusion than the toe of her sandal caught on an exposed root and she pitched forward, landing hard on her hands and knees. Chris was beside her before she even got her breath back, his hands strong on her shoulders as he helped her to her feet.

''Are you okay?''

She nodded, gulping as she brushed the debris off her culottes and her bare knees. That was the first time he had been that close to her, or touched her, since yesterday afternoon. His nearness was more unsettling than the fall had been.

"I tripped. Should have been watching my feet, I guess."

He released her shoulders and stepped back, frowning as he looked down at her feet. "Those shoes are about worthless."

"I didn't know I'd be hiking through the jungle when I got dressed yesterday." The absence of his touch, the note of irritability that had crept into his voice, made her response a little sharper than it should have been, and she shrugged in quick, uncomfortable apology. "Anyway, I can stand a few blisters for one day."

"Unfortunately it's going to take a lot longer than one day to get where we're going." He was still frowning as he looked at her purse. "I don't suppose you brought a pair of socks, did you? That would protect your feet some anyway."

But she barely registered his question. "What do you mean, it's going to take more than one day? You said it was twenty miles. If we walk three miles per hour—"

"Three miles? Honey, I'd be very much surprised if we've covered a quarter of a mile in the last hour and the going's going to get a lot rougher. What gave you an idea like that? We'd be lucky to make it across the island on horseback in one day, much less on foot."

"Do you mean..." her voice was hoarse "...we're going to have to spend the night here?"

She didn't like the way he avoided her eyes. "At least."

"What are you talking about? How long do you think it's going to take?"

Still he wouldn't look at her. "A couple of days, maybe. Depending on whether we come up against something unexpected."

Lanie stared at him. "What do you mean, unexpected?"

"Come on. The less time we waste the sooner we'll be out of here."

"What do you mean, *unexpected?*"

But he was already moving ahead, pushing back branches and trampling down undergrowth, and Lanie had to hurry, almost tripping again, just to keep up.

It was close to noon when she discovered what he meant by "unexpected."

By that time they had been walking close to five hours with only one or two brief breaks for carefully rationed sips of mineral water, and Lanie was hot, sweaty and exhausted. Under the best of conditions she would not have enjoyed a five-hour hike. Her feet were blistered, her shoulder was raw from the weight of her purse, and she was starving. If Chris didn't call a halt for lunch soon she would insist they stop.

He was about five long strides ahead of her when suddenly he stopped. Lanie closed the distance between them at her own pace, kicking at the thin vines that threatened to entangle themselves in the straps of her sandals and dragging her purse. She drew up beside him and saw why he had stopped.

Before him the ground began to slope sharply, culminating in a twenty-foot drop into a gully.

For a moment she was so stunned and overwhelmed that she couldn't even speak. When at last the words came they were hopelessly foolish, the product of utter fatigue and complete disbelief. "We can't cross that!"

The grim lines that bracketed his mouth momentarily deepened. "I know."

The banks of the fissure were almost vertical and covered with a thick creeping vine that could have concealed almost anything. Rocky protrusions and spiny bushes stuck out at a ninety-degree angle, so that a slip of the foot could result in a serious injury at the very least. And even if they managed to reach the bottom of the gully there was no way they could get up the opposite bank. The gully went on in either direction as far as she could see, and in places seemed to be even deeper. She could not have been at more of a loss, more stunned and defeated. They'd walked all morning—plowed through the jungle in sticky tropical heat, been clawed by nettles and stung by insects—only to come up on a dead end.

"We'll have to find a way to get around," she heard Chris say.

"No." She shook her head. "Oh, no. We can walk the rest of the day and never find a way around it."

"It's got to shallow out somewhere."

"Why? Why does it? Why can't it just go all the way across, a big crack in the middle of the island? No." She pronounced the single word with firm, decisive finality. "We're going back to the beach. We never should have left in the first place."

His tone was dismissive. "Don't be ridiculous, we're not turning back. It looks to me like the easiest going will be to the east—"

"You can go east if you want to," Lanie replied, hitching the strap of her purse over her shoulder again. "I'm going back."

She turned with every intention of doing just that, and he must have seen then that she was serious because he grabbed her arm. "Are you crazy? You don't even know which way 'back' is!"

"Well, guess what?" Coolly, she disengaged her arm. "I'll either find it or I won't, and if I die trying you can have me on your conscience because I'm not going one step deeper into this jungle."

Impatience flashed in his eyes. "Great. Perfect female logic. Almost as sensible as sitting on the beach tossing out distress messages in bottles and waiting for somebody to pick one up. Or maybe we could write SOS in the sand with shells?''

"I never said that. I never said anything *like* that! And I can do without your putting stupid words in my mouth!''

"Of course you can. You do that well enough without any help from me.''

Lanie whirled to stalk away from him.

"Damn it, Lanie, will you for God's sake be reasonable? We've been walking all morning and now you want to turn *back?* It'll be dark before we get back to the beach and then what will be have?''

"A chance!'' she cried. "Which is a hell of a lot more than we have rotting away out here in this steam bath—''

"A chance for what? Severe exposure? Starvation?''

"No one would ever even think to look for us here! At least on the beach if someone came by—''

"No one is going to come by! Will you get that through your head once and for all? The beach on the north side of the island isn't even on any of the navigational maps, no one would have any *reason* to come by! And even if I'm wrong, even if the good fairy who watches over stranded sailors sends a magical rescue boat, just what are we supposed to do for food and water while we're waiting? Because what's in this picnic bag isn't going to last forever, I can promise you that.''

"We could fish, or dig clams or—I don't know! At least we'd know where we *were!*''

"Which wouldn't do a whole hell of a lot of good if we're the *only* ones who know it, now would it?'' He drew a sharp breath through his teeth, averting his eyes for what was obviously the time it took to regain his composure. When he spoke again it was in a slightly calmer tone. "Look, Lanie, we can't go on arguing like this. It's wasting time and energy we don't have to spare. Someone has got to be in charge.''

"And you vote for you I suppose.''

The flesh around his eyes tightened. "Do you have a problem with that?''

"Why should I?'' Her voice was growing shrill, but she couldn't help it. "You did such a terrific job getting us here! Why, if it weren't for you we might have actually *landed* on the south side of the island—you know, where the food and the radio and the buildings are? Where boats are *supposed* to land?''

"For God's sake, Lanie, what the hell do you expect me to *do*?''

"How should I know? Build a damn boat! That's what you're supposed to be good at, aren't you?''

"And maybe you'd like to navigate by the stars—then at least *you'd* be good for something!''

The surge of fury robbed Lanie of words, and this time when she strode away she didn't look back.

For a moment Chris was tempted to let her go. Let her get lost, let her come crying to him, let her take care of herself for a while. But then with a bitten-back oath he shrugged off the picnic bag and plunged after her. "Damn it, Lanie, if you think I'm going to spend the rest of the day chasing you through the jungle—"

His legs were longer than hers and he caught up with her in only a few strides. But he hadn't counted on how mad she was, and when he grabbed her arm she turned on him like a banshee. She tried to swing her purse at him, but he ducked. She gave a low growling scream of fury and kicked his shin just as he grabbed her other arm to ward off a blow. He jerked her forward as she twisted back and they both lost their balance, falling hard on the jungle floor.

Cursing, Chris got to a sitting position as she bucked and wriggled beneath him, flailing at him with her fists. He pinned her legs between his knees and caught her wrists, angrily forcing them over her head and out of his way. And then she was beneath him, her face flushed, her eyes blazing, her chest heaving.

Her skin was shiny with sweat, a damp triangle darkened her tank top between her breasts and he could see the shape of her nipples, upthrust by the position in which he had pinned her hands. The heat from her body was steamy, her muscles taut and poised, her breathing quick. Chris's heartbeat, once rapid from exertion, became slow and heavy, filling up his chest, and he felt himself grow hard.

A single push of his hand would bare those breasts to him. Another low tearing motion would bring her pelvis against his. One thrust and he would be inside her. He was very still, and so was she.

A drop of sweat rolled down his cheek and splashed on her throat. He could see her pulse, quick and fast. Fear or desire? Hate or need? And did it matter?

He was suddenly shaken by a surge of shame and self disgust and he rolled off of her, pulling her roughly to her feet with him. *We're not animals,* he thought, but that was the only clear thought in his head. *We're not.* He released her quickly, before she had her balance and stumbled against him, but then backed away before he could touch her again.

He looked at her and didn't know what to say. He turned and walked back to where he had left the picnic bag.

Lanie drew a deep breath, trying to calm her shattered nerves. She could still feel his hands on her, the strength of his muscles, the heat of his breath. And she could still feel her reaction to him, pounding in her veins. How had everything gotten so turned around? And how could everything keep going so wrong?

"I guess," she said after a moment, "we could try going east."

He pulled a bottle of water from the picnic bag and started to drink, then offered it to her. She shook her head.

After another moment she said, with an effort, "I never actually read *Lord of the Flies*. What happened?"

He finished drinking from the bottle and replaced the cap. "These kids were stranded on a desert island, started turning into savages. They ended up trying to kill each other, I think."

Lanie swallowed hard. "Well. We'll try not to let it come to that."

"Yeah." His voice was glum. Or perhaps just tired. "Are you hungry?"

"Not really." Not anymore.

"Me, either. But we'd better eat before we go on."

They did not take much time to make a meal. Lanie was afraid to sit on the ground—she could not even think about making her bed there—so she spread some cheese between two pieces of bread and ate it standing up. Chris sat down with his back against a tree and ate in an absent, preoccupied fashion. Neither of them referred, by word or gesture, to what had happened between them. There was nothing to say.

When Lanie couldn't stand the silence any longer she said, "Why did they take the tender?"

For a moment he looked as though he hadn't heard her. He focused his attention on her with an effort that was more polite than interested. "What do you mean?"

"It's been bothering me all morning. If they just wanted to steal the *Serendipity,* why didn't they just take off as soon as we were out of sight? Why steal the tender too?"

Chris frowned, obviously intrigued.

Encouraged, Lanie went on. "Look at it another way. If they had left the tender, what would you have done? Would you have used it to go after them?"

"Of course not. I never could've caught them and it would've been dangerous to take a boat that size out on the open seas."

"But you *could* have used it to get around the island, couldn't you? To the company complex?"

"And the radio. And the first thing I would've done would be to report the theft."

"But by that time would it have really done any good? I mean how could you have known what course they were taking and how many helicopters could the coast guard put up to look for it?" She hesitated, not sure herself where the train of thought was leading. "I'm just wondering if it really would have made that much difference, as far as their getaway was concerned."

"Do you mean the point was not so much to steal the *Serendipity* but to leave us here to die?"

The quick and callous way in which he reached that conclusion gave Lanie a chill. She shook her head. "No, I don't think they meant to hurt us...or at least not badly. Otherwise Joel wouldn't have made sure we had food and water. And the other thing is, what were they going to *do* with the *Serendipity?*"

There was surprise in Chris's eyes, and also curiosity.

"I mean, it's not like a Buick, that they can switch the plates on and repaint and sell to the highest bidder. Is it?"

Chris's frown deepened thoughtfully. It was good to see him frown not with anger or anxiety, but simple intellectual curiosity. "Maybe. It doesn't make a whole lot of sense, when you think about it. On the other hand..." the frown sharpened briefly with a dismissive shrug "...there's no law that says criminals have to make sense."

But Lanie could tell he was thinking about it, and for the first time since they had been stranded the worry that tautened his face took the background to a less immediate and far less threatening problem. It wasn't much, and Lanie was not at all sure what it meant, but some of the strain between them seemed to ease.

CHRIS WAS RIGHT: the gully did grow shallower as they moved east, although they both knew it was luck more than skill that caused him to choose the right direction. Late in the afternoon they were able to cross, though not without incident. Chris slipped going down the incline and scraped several inches of skin off his shin. Lanie missed a handhold climbing up the other side and fell backwards four feet to the bottom.

After that it was clear both of them were too tired to go much farther. Lanie did not argue when Chris decided they would stop for the night just on the other side of the gully.

Throughout the day the ground cover had varied from thick and viny to sparse and sandy; Chris walked a few hundred yards and found a spot that was more sand than vines and began to spread out the blankets.

"There's not enough dry wood around here to make a fire," he said. "But it's warmer away from the beach and there's no wind. I think we'll be okay."

Lanie looked at the ground surrounding the blankets uneasily. "There could be snakes."

He glanced at her. "There aren't any snakes."

"Maybe not now. Maybe you just didn't see them. But they could crawl up anytime and we wouldn't see them in the dark."

"I suppose." He took the second blanket from the picnic bag and opened it with a snap.

"And bugs." She looked anxiously at the dense growth of overhead foliage and the thick viny leaves that surrounded them. "Those leaves are probably thick with bugs."

"Probably."

"Spiders, and those awful palmetto bugs that are as big as dinner plates—"

"Good. If we can catch enough, we might be *having* them for dinner."

"I'm serious."

"You think I'm not?"

"I can't sleep on the ground with the bugs and the snakes!"

"Where do you want to sleep, in the trees?"

"Well, couldn't you rig up a hammock or something out of the—"

"No," he said, and so sharply that Lanie actually took a startled step backward. His eyes were filled with venom as he turned on her. "No, I can't, okay? I *can't.*"

"Well what *can* you do? I mean, you're the dashing pirate, aren't you? Don't you think it might have been smart of you to figure out where we were going to sleep before you decided we should spend the night in the jungle?"

"Damn it, Lanie, don't start with me—"

"You? What about *me?* I followed you, didn't I? I've done everything you said. If you'd listened to me we'd be on the beach now—there aren't any snakes on the beach! But no, I listened to you, I let you lead us deeper into the jungle and get bitten by ants and scratched by thorns and exposed to God knows how much poison ivy because you said you knew what you were doing! But this is it, this is too much. You can't make me do this anymore!''

The look he gave her was incredulity laced with contempt. "So what are you going to do, call the auto club? Face it, lady, I'm all you've got and like it or not we're stuck with each other. And if you think this is my idea of a luxury vacation—"

"Yes!" she cried. "Yes, I do. I think you've probably spent your whole life just waiting for a chance like this, stranded on a deserted island, living off the land, playing pirate king. I think you're enjoying this! It's all just another fantasy to you!"

The look he gave her was distant and disdainful, laced with cold fire. "If you really believe that," he told her, "you're even crazier than I thought. Because believe me, when I have fantasies I'm a lot more choosy about who I bring along for the ride."

Acid tears stung her eyes. She turned quickly away to hide them but couldn't stop them from spilling over. And she couldn't stop Chris from seeing.

Furiously she pressed her fists to her eyes, refusing to give in to the weakness. She could feel Chris watching her, and that only made it harder.

"Lanie, I'm sorry."

She heard him take a step toward her and she held up a hand to ward him off, her back still to him. "I know. It's okay."

She knelt on the blanket and started to unpack the remaining food in the picnic basket, but the tears kept blurring her vision. When Chris knelt behind her and put his hands on her shoulders she lost the battle and sobs shook her shoulders. He drew her gently against his chest and let her cry.

At first she cried from fear and fatigue and worry and dread and she hated herself for crying; the last thing she had wanted to be before Chris was a helpless hysterical woman. Then she cried from anger because the last thing she wanted to be *at all* was here in this place and it wasn't fair, none of it was fair. And then she realized she was really crying because she needed Chris so badly, needed to be held by him, needed to be close to him, and everything she did only pushed him farther away. Even in his arms she was alone.

Chris held her as her tears gave way to exhaustion, and though she wanted to apologize she didn't have the energy. He pushed her hair away from her wet, hot face and said quietly, "Hell of a day, huh?" She simply nodded in mute gratitude for his understanding, and allowed herself one more moment in his embrace before moving away, strengthening her muscles, returning to the chore she had left behind.

She knew she couldn't make her voice normal and didn't try. It sounded thick and muffled as she said, "Can we drink the rest of the wine? Are you saving it?"

"No. Finish it. We'll need the bottle in case we find water."

Lanie poured a generous measure into one of yesterday's glasses.

"God, Lanie, I'm sorry for getting you into this," Chris said abruptly. "You have every right to blame me, but please believe me it's the last thing I wanted."

She turned to look at him, and the expression on his face broke her heart. "Oh Chris," she said softly, looking down into the glass she held with both hands. "I don't blame you. That's not why I was crying. I just..." She raised her eyes to him, pleading. "I just don't want you to hate me. I don't want to be left out here alone."

The denial that sprang to his face was swift and genuine. "I don't hate you. And I'd never leave you alone!"

"You already have." And as understanding slowly came to his face she felt her heart twist in her chest. It was the saddest thing she had ever seen. "Oh Chris, what happened to us? We had a stupid argument—"

"Not stupid," he said quietly. "You were right, Lanie. I was playing games with your emotions and I had no right. Maybe I'd convinced myself otherwise but I couldn't have offered you anything once we left the *Serendipity*...." His lips twisted into a bitter smile. "As you can see, my sphere of influence does not extend to deserted tropical islands or suburban wastelands."

Then he lifted his shoulders in a resigned gesture. "You wanted to know what kind of man I'd be in the real world, and you had a right to wonder. I guess I did, too. Well..." he made a palms-up gesture that indicated their surroundings "...this is it. What do you think?"

She didn't know what to say to him. She didn't know how to take back all her harsh words and ugly accusations, she didn't know how to tell him that she still needed him, more desperately now than ever before, as her friend if not her lover. She didn't know how to tell him how much she blamed herself, how much she hated herself, for what they had lost.

So she told him the simple truth.

"I think," she said, and raised her glass to him, "that there's not another person in the world I'd rather be stranded on a desert island with."

His smile was slow in coming, but it was genuine. It made her heart catch, until she saw the shadows that still haunted his eyes. "You know something? Me, too."

They shared that moment, a smile, a cautious warmth, and slowly, almost inevitably, the barriers between them began to soften and to yield. And just as inevitably the air between them began to warm, the resonance of awareness that had always been there like background music began to swell, filling each breath and echoing in every heartbeat.

The width of the blanket separated them, but one outstretched arm could have brought them together. Lanie could feel the brush of Chris's gaze across her lips and her throat and her breasts, like the stroke of a gentle hand. She could taste him, she could feel the warmth of his sinewy muscles enfolding her. She could feel her legs entwining with his, his hard length stretching over her, his fingers closing around hers...but only in her mind, because what had once been between them would never be the same again. She raised her eyes to his, her heartbeat slow and heavy with expectation, uncertainty and hope, and she saw the same kind of need there, the low fierce fire of physical desire—and the same kind of sorrow, confusion and loss.

Sex, like everything else, had once been so easy between them. A game, a thrilling entertainment, adventure without risk. But this was an entirely different world, and the rules had changed. They weren't even the same people they had been twenty-four hours ago, and this was not a game.

His eyes moved to the food she had set out and to the jungle around them. His voice sounded strained as he said, "Lanie, I'm really tired. I think I'll stretch out for a while."

Lanie nodded and swallowed back her hurt. "Sure. I'll just put this stuff away so it doesn't attract bugs. You'll be hungry later."

Their eyes met for another moment and she thought he might say something else, but she wasn't at all sure she wanted to hear. She turned quickly and began to repack the bag. Chris lay down on his blanket, his forearm shielding his eyes.

When she was done she sat alone, sipping the wine, hoarding the precious moments of daylight. Chris lay still, counting his heartbeats, trying not to look at her.

He thought about the capricious nature of desire, its ebb and flow. He thought about power, just as deceptive by nature, just as inconstant. If he could have lifted his hand and erased the events of the past twenty-four hours he would have. If he could have taken her in his arms and made love to her until she forgot her fear and his betrayal, he would have done so. But that kind of power he did not have.

He turned his head to look at her. She was sitting in profile to him, the hand that held the glass resting on one updrawn knee. The slender length of her arm, the curve of her breast as molded by the soft material of the tank top, the line of her thigh where her culottes fell away, the evening shadows that planed her face, the shape of her fingers as they curved around the glass... Every part of her was more appealing than ever before, and yet never had a woman seemed quite so far away, so out of his reach.

He could open his arms to her and she would come. He could kiss her and she would respond, eagerly; the passion would flare and she would welcome it. Their coupling would be wild and frantic. His body would drive into hers and hers would consume his and for that moment they could push aside the fear, blot out the horrors of the day, pretend the emptiness was filled. But when it was over, nothing would be changed. She would still be a stranger, and he would still have nothing to offer her. They would still be lost in the jungle with nothing to depend on but each other, and a few moments' desperate passion would not make anything better for either of them.

He wished it could be different; he wished he could *make* it different. But he couldn't.

He wondered if she would sit up all night, afraid of the bugs and the snakes. There was so little he could do for her now, but perhaps they could each make the night pass a little easier for the other.

When he spoke he could tell his voice startled her, soft as it was.

"Lanie," he said, "I'm exhausted, I'm filthy, and I hurt all over. Will you come lie with me anyway, and keep me warm?"

Lanie turned, and he was holding out his hand to her. Understanding came slowly, and with it quiet gratitude. She carefully poured the remainder of the wine back into the bottle, recorked it, and crept wordlessly into his arms.

They held each other as the day died, not speaking, not caressing, just taking comfort in each other's strength.

"It's never going to be the same between us, is it?" Lanie asked in a quiet voice.

His lips touched her hair lightly. "No," he said, "it's not. But maybe it will be better."

Chapter Nine

Day two.

They were lost, and Chris was not surprised. The trees grew taller as they moved farther in, the undergrowth thicker, and at times it was difficult to even see the sun, much less steer by it. The night had been warmer than the one spent on the beach and their shared body heat had helped, but they both had awakened with coughs.

Chris had never before imagined that he could sleep with a woman he found as desirable as he did Lanie and do nothing but that—sleep. But in this alien, hostile environment he was discovering a great many things about himself he had never imagined before.

The unaccustomed exercise had restored lost appetites and they were both hungry, particularly since they had decided to dispose of the chicken. Neither one of them knew how long the meat would last unrefrigerated, and food poisoning could be deadly under these conditions. But it wasn't the food that worried Chris so much as the water. They had three small bottles of mineral water and perhaps a cup of wine left.

He asked himself what Grandpa Hannibal would do, and the answer was simple: keep moving.

Chris had found a long, relatively sturdy stick that he used as a staff to clear the way of as much undergrowth as he could. Already he had sent two snakes slithering out of the way, but he did not mention that to Lanie. He didn't like to think about it much himself.

He was about three strides ahead of her when he heard her gasp. Perhaps because he was thinking about the snakes the sound went through him with an icy stab of alarm, but before he had even finished turning, her gasp had become a choked cry.

Lanie staggered backward, one hand pressed against her neck, her face contorted with pain. Chris was on her in an instant, grabbing her shoulders, demanding, "What? What is it?"

"Nothing—just a bee, I guess. *God,* it hurts."

Chris wanted to feel relief but the tightness of her face, the shakiness of her voice, wouldn't let him. "Let me see."

Her fingers were stiff and she stifled another cry as he pried them away from her neck. The wound was almost directly over her collarbone, angry red with a white center, like a bee sting, but already swollen to a noticeable degree. He demanded hoarsely, "Are you allergic?" When she didn't answer right away he gripped her shoulders hard and practically shouted, "Lanie, *are you allergic?*"

She shook her head, but her voice sounded weak and high as she answered, "No, I—I just never knew a bee sting could could hurt so much."

Her teeth were chattering. It was eighty degrees and her face was filmed with sweat, but she was shivering. Chris could hear his own blood rushing in his ears as he slipped an arm around her waist for support. Was it his imagination, or was she breathing harder? The sudden parchment pallor of her face was not his imagination, nor was the clamminess of her skin. "Yeah, I know. Maybe you'd better sit down."

She took a step forward and sagged against him. Her purse slid off her shoulder and onto the ground. She said in a small shaky voice, "Chris, I don't...I feel like I'm going to be sick."

"It's okay, honey. You're okay...."

But she wasn't, and Chris's heart was slamming in his chest, hurting his ribs, then it seemed to stop altogether as Lanie went limp against him. He caught her before she fell and hardly felt her weight as he lifted her against his chest.

Terror was swift and sharp and total, and the next few seconds were like blank-screen flashes in a fast-moving slide show. He laid her on the ground and her face was still and white; her head rolled limply to the side and he couldn't tell whether she was breathing. He pressed his fingers frantically against her throat but he couldn't feel a pulse and he kept hearing a voice that whispered, "God Lanie, don't do this, please honey, don't..." It was a long time before he realized that voice was his.

He pressed his face against her chest, just below her left breast, he squeezed his eyes shut and stilled his own breath and his prayer was wordless and desperate until, through the screaming roar of his own pulse he heard her heartbeat, quick and light, and he felt the rise and fall of her chest.

"Okay, sweetheart, that's good, hold on...."

He sat up, smoothing her hair back from her face with both hands in a single firm desperate motion. Her skin was like ice, pallid and damp, her breathing rapid and shallow. When he touched her she moaned softly and her eyelids fluttered, but did not open. The swelling over her collarbone was the size of a lemon.

He left her for a moment to retrieve the picnic bag from where he had dropped it, tearing it open when the zipper jammed. He pulled out a blanket and wrapped her in it, then grabbed her purse and up-ended it, scattering the contents over the ground. Scissors, hairbrush, various tubes and vials and packets and pouches... He pushed through the items with the mad desperate haste of a junkie in search of a fix, but all he could find was a bottle of aspirin and a blister pack of cold capsules.

He tore at the blister pack and spilled several of the capsules on the ground. His fingers felt as big as sausages as he tried to pick them up. *God, let this be the right thing to do....* His hands were shaking so badly that he spilled half a bottle of precious water on the ground as he poured a small measure into a cup, then broke open one of the capsules into it. After a moment's hesitation he spilled another capsule into the mixture and turned back to Lanie.

Her eyes were half-open but unfocused. She murmured, "Chris?" And it was a thick, uncoordinated syllable. There were patches of terrifyingly bright color under her cheekbones and on her throat.

"Yes, sweetheart, I'm here. It's okay, you're going to be okay." He got his arm beneath her shoulder and lifted her to a half-sitting position in his lap, cradling her head against his chest. "Can you drink this? Try to swallow it."

He could tell it was hard for her to swallow and his own throat constricted with anxiety. *Please.* But she got the medicine down and lay still against his chest, her lashes casting dark shadows in the hollows beneath her eyes. He watched her closely, hardly daring to breathe himself, stroking her forehead. He could still feel the occasional chill wrack her body, even beneath the blanket, but her breathing seemed slower and heavier. He wasn't sure whether that was a good thing.

Her brow wrinkled with effort, or with pain, and she whispered, "Wh—what did you give me?"

"Cold medicine." His own voice was hoarse. "An antihistamine."

And God knows what else... "It should help you breathe, and take down the swelling."

"It really hurts...."

"I know, honey." He touched her cheek with his lips. "I know it does. I'm sorry."

He could see her struggling with the pain and every deep shaking breath she took was like the stab of a knife in his own chest. He didn't want to leave her so he stretched across her for the aspirin bottle, grasping it with his middle two fingers. The child-proof cap frustrated him and he ended up removing it with his teeth. He shook a handful of the tablets into his palm, hesitated a moment, then popped them into his mouth, chewing them into thick paste, which he then applied to the swollen sting wound on Lanie's collarbone.

She opened her eyes, mumbling, "What are you doing?"

"You don't want to know. You probably won't find it in any approved medical text, but it might make you feel better."

Another chill wracked her body. "God, I'm so cold."

He draped the second blanket over her and wrapped his arms and legs around her, rubbing her icy hands between his. It came to him then, the words he had been trying to ignore, fighting to avoid, a truth as stark and unforgiving as the jungle itself, a cold dank breath brushing across the back of his neck: *She could die.* He closed his eyes and he held her tightly, as though he could form a physical barrier between her and the insidious poison whose source he couldn't even identify, as though through sheer force of will he could link one beat of her heart to the other. *Lanie, don't die....*

Maybe it was a lifetime he held her, maybe it was an hour. The shivering stopped, and her breathing seemed easier. The brightly colored patches on her cheeks and throat began to fade. She pushed fitfully at the blankets as her temperature returned to normal. She seemed to doze.

He made her as comfortable as he could, rolling their two jackets together to form a pillow for her head, leaving one blanket draped over her lightly. He got up and walked away, just a few steps, and stood with his arms folded across his chest, breathing deeply, staring into the jungle.

He thought about how quickly it could come, between one step and the next, without warning or preamble, swift and final. No chance to argue or persuade or wheedle or charm, no recounts allowed. The strike of the snake, the bite of the spider, the bolt of lightning from a clear blue sky... the heart that quit too soon. It didn't have to be fair or easy or right; no guarantees were issued. Why had no one ever told him that?

"Chris?"

He was with her in two steps, dropping to one knee beside her. "How do you feel?"

She swallowed with a visible wince. "Like I'm just getting over the flu. Achy, dizzy. Stupid." She touched the nodule on her collarbone which, beneath the aspirin poultice, had shrunk considerably, and her wince was sharper. "Wow. What was it?"

He shook his head. Relief spread through his tightly knotted muscles in cautious spirals. "Some kind of fast-acting poisonous bite. Fortunately not deadly." He forced a smile. "Can you wiggle your fingers and toes? Everything still working?"

She nodded, and her smile, weak though it was, went straight to his heart.

He brushed her bangs back from her forehead. Her skin was still damp, but its temperature neutral. His voice was a little husky as he said, "If I could remember even half the bargains I made over the past hour or so I'd be a candidate for sainthood."

She lifted her fingers to touch his. "As far as I'm concerned, you already are."

He closed his fingers around hers, and he could barely make his voice work for the next words. "I don't want to lose you, Lanie."

He didn't want to lose her smile or the light in those soft brown eyes or her stubbornness or her wit. He didn't want to lose her to fast-acting poison or an infected cut or contaminated water... or to Camden, Iowa or his stupidity. He wanted to tell her that, but he didn't know where to start. Maybe she saw it in his face because she squeezed his fingers and deepened her smile, though he could tell it hurt her to do so.

"I know what you mean," she said. "Burying a body in this jungle would be no fun at all, would it?"

He took his cue from her and returned the smile. "Don't make me find out, okay?"

"No danger of that. You make a pretty good nurse. Where did a city boy like you learn all that anyway?"

He tried to keep his tone casual as he reached for the overturned picnic bag and retrieved the bottle of wine. "I studied a little first aid. You have to, to get your certification. But I learned about bee stings..." He uncorked the bottle and brought it to his lips, drinking deeply "...because my brother was allergic. He took shots once a week for ten years."

"Well, I'm sorry about your brother, but glad you were around when I needed someone who knew about antihistamine. Pretty smart."

"No." He drank from the bottle again. "Smart would have been to stay on the beach."

"Chris..." She struggled to sit up but had only lifted her head a few inches before the color drained from her face and she sank down again, fighting an obvious battle with nausea.

Chris shifted quickly to take her head in his lap, cradling her face with his hands. "Take it easy. I think you've gone as far as you're going for today."

She lay with her eyes closed, drawing slow deep breaths through parted lips. After a time she managed, "We're really lost, aren't we?"

It was a moment before Chris could reply. "Lost is a relative term." Then he abandoned the effort at lightness and answered simply, "Yeah. We're lost."

She was silent for a long time. She turned her head, resting her cheek against his thigh, and he combed his fingers gently through her hair. "How long will it be before they miss you, and send someone to look for you?"

Chris's hand paused in its movement through her hair. There was a hollow feeling in the pit of his stomach as he thought back on his last conversation with Madison, a lifetime ago, in another world. "I don't know. Months maybe."

She turned her head, looking up at him, her dark pained eyes now shadowed with puzzlement as well.

"But, you're an important person. I thought you said you had a board meeting."

He shook his head slowly. "It wouldn't be the first one I've missed." His voice was heavy, underscored with the bitter edge of self-accusation. "I'm not known for my sense of responsibility, and the last thing I said to Madison was to expect me when she saw me."

Lanie moistened her lips, drawing a deep breath. "Well," she said, "I guess this is where you say if you had it all to do over again you'd do it differently."

"You got that right." The fervor with which he spoke surprised even him, and he found himself wondering if he was even capable of doing things differently. He hoped he would get a chance to find out.

He looked down at her, aching with regret. "I would guess that you can think of a few things you'd like to have a chance to do differently, too."

She lowered her lashes and pressed her lips together, and he thought she was biting back harsh words that he no doubt deserved. Then she looked up at him again, briefly and a little shyly. "No...I'm afraid if I changed anything about my life, even the bad things, it might keep me from meeting you. And..." she smiled "...in spite of everything, you're still the most fun I've ever had."

Chris wanted her then, with a sudden fierce intensity that left him light-headed. He wanted to bury himself inside her and draw her inside his pores, to feel her in every part of him and to possess every part of her, for it was not just a physical wanting. It went to the very core of his soul, and its mere power left him shaken.

He pushed his fingers through the hair at her temples, giving himself time to regain his voice. But even then his voice was husky as he said, "You're a little crazy, do you know that?"

"That's the nicest thing you've said to me in two days, do you know that?"

Give me a chance, Chris thought. *Give me a chance to make it up to you. Give me a lifetime.*

Instead he said, "Next time you want some attention, just ask. There's no need for the life-and-death theatrics."

"I'll try to remember that."

But the remorse that went through him was swift and sharp and he could not maintain the humor any longer. "Lanie, I'm—"

She wouldn't let him finish. "I've been thinking about how much worse it could have been. I mean, what if we'd been shipwrecked, with no life raft and sharks circling?"

He stared at her for a moment, then he understood what she was trying to do. He hesitated, then took another sip from the bottle, forcing his muscles to relax. "That would have been worse," he agreed.

"At least we had the picnic basket and the blankets. And you know the island. You knew about the cliffs. We could have started walking around the beach and had to turn back and by that time our water would be gone, so it could have been worse. And there is shelter on the island, and warehouses full of food...."

"They've got freezers big enough to drive a truck into," he mused, "and all of them crammed full of steaks and ribs and hamburger." He glanced at her apologetically. "Maybe we'd better not talk about the freezers."

"Agreed."

He sipped from the bottle again. "I've been thinking about what you said yesterday. And maybe you were right. Maybe the point wasn't to steal the *Serendipity,* but to hurt me."

She looked up at him, her eyes wide. "Why would anyone want to do that?"

He looked out into the jungle as though searching for the answer. "I don't know," he admitted. "I don't like to think of myself as having enemies—which is exactly why I'm not a very good leader."

Her brows knitted in puzzlement. "What do you mean?"

"Did you ever wonder what kind of king Prince Charming made?" He lifted the bottle again. "You can't be a good administrator and win a popularity contest at the same time. I guess I've always known that, but never cared. Running the company was just something to do to pass the time." He shrugged. "I don't know. I guess I must've done something to make someone mad while I wasn't paying attention, because you're right—there's more than a stolen yacht at stake here. Someone wanted me out of the way."

"Then it wasn't my fault," Lanie said slowly.

He looked at her, surprised. "What?"

"You only came ashore because of me," she explained. "If I hadn't been on board you never would have gotten off and—"

He started shaking his head with her first words, amazed. "Is *that* what you've been thinking? Honey, if they meant to get rid of me they would have done it, if not at this port then in Nassau or Bimini or on the open sea. The original plan might have been a lot more violent than just leaving me stranded. Your being aboard might have saved my life."

She smiled, and he experienced a shaft of surprised admiration for the deft way in which she had manipulated the conversation. "Then I guess maybe we're even, because so far I think you've been a great leader. And if they meant to leave us stranded they would have found a way to do it even if we'd come ashore on the south side of the island, wouldn't they?"

He returned her smile with a rueful shake of his head. "I suppose."

But then the gentle humor in her eyes faded into seriousness, and she said simply, "No one would have found us if we'd stayed on the beach, Chris."

Their gazes held for a long solemn moment of quiet understanding. As clearly and precisely as though an invisible curtain had dropped, dividing one part of their relationship from the other, everything between them was changed.

He stroked her forehead tenderly and said, "You're tired. Why don't you try to sleep?"

"I am tired," she admitted. "You talk for a while." She shifted her head more comfortably on his knee. "Tell me about this Madison person."

He hesitated, then laughed. He took another drink from the bottle. "Now *there's* a story."

Chapter Ten

Day Four.

If anyone had told Lanie two weeks ago that she could go four days without washing her underwear she would have been beyond amazement. Now there were so many things to be genuinely amazed over that a little thing like clean underwear was an almost unimaginable luxury, its absence hardly worth noticing.

First and foremost was her amazement over the fact that they were still here, lost in the jungle, still moving, still alive. Sometimes it almost seemed as though movement were the end unto itself, as though it didn't even matter where they ended up or what they were moving toward as long as they kept moving.

She was amazed that they had spent three nights sleeping on the jungle floor and had survived with nothing more serious than a few itchy ant bites. After her previous close call, both of them should have been terrified of the things that crawled along the jungle floor or crept through the trees or flew from leaf to leaf, but in fact the incident had had the opposite effect. They viewed the dangers that surrounded them with awareness and respect, but wasted no energy on fearing what they couldn't change. That amazed Lanie, too, when she bothered to think about it.

What amazed her even more was that she could sleep every night in Chris's arms and do nothing more than sleep.

At midmorning they came upon a deadfall of sorts—the remnants of a storm that had tossed small trees and bamboo canes into a ragged heap too wide to go around, too unstable to climb. Chris surveyed it for a moment, hands on hips, then said, "Well, just in case you were getting bored . . ."

"I wasn't," she assured him.

He let the picnic bag slide to the ground and grabbed hold of the trunk of a broken sapling, tugging it free of vines and entanglements, and dragging it aside. After a moment Lanie went forward to help. He smiled at her in an easy, companionable way and took hold of another branch, muscles tensing as he lifted and tossed it aside. Lanie's heart seemed to spiral to her throat and melt there, just from his smile. Just from looking at him.

The beard that covered the lower part of his face was still sparse, reddish colored and prickly looking, but it gave his face a leaner, harder look that sometimes took Lanie by surprise with its raw masculinity. She knew his hair couldn't really have grown in the past four days but it seemed longer. He had torn a strip from the bottom of his T-shirt to use as a sweatband and to keep his hair out of his face. Lanie found it oddly sexy. He'd always been a lean, athletic-looking man, but his muscles seemed to have grown longer and harder over the past few days of erratic diet and strenuous exercise. Now there was a primitive strength about him that she'd never noticed before.

When he bent to lift a heavy branch, the tendons in his neck corded and the veins on his forearms stood out and Lanie was gripped, suddenly and unexpectedly, by a wave of lust so intense it made her stomach cramp. She had to look quickly away, turning her attention to a tangle of bamboo that was blocking part of a broken tree Chris was trying to dislodge.

"So," he said, grunting a little, "where were we?"

Whether it was out of some barely acknowledged need to remind themselves of who they had once been in the lives they had left behind or simply a way to distract themselves from the hunger, the thirst and the aching muscles, they had talked constantly. And they learned more about each other in the last forty-eight hours than most people did in a lifetime.

Chris had started it with, "Tell me a story, Lanie." And she did, about her nephew Brian as a baby, her niece, her sister and her brother, and before she knew it her entire family was spread out before him with all their foibles and imperfections; their secrets were his.

The bamboo she'd been wrestling with came free with a suddenness that caused her to stumble backward. She paused to catch her breath, blotting her forehead with the back of her arm. "Nephews and nieces," she replied. "They were out of the cute stage and into the horrid stage—I think that's the one that lasts the rest of their lives. So no more precious anecdotes."

He watched as she moved back to the deadfall, grasping a protruding branch, bracing her feet to tug it loose. A week ago she wouldn't have come near a viny, snake-like mess like this, much less put her hands into it. A week ago, of course, he wouldn't have allowed her to. She had changed, and so had he.

She had lost weight over the past few days—they both had—so that the waistband of her culottes now rested just above her hipbones, and he followed the slim line of her torso to the flare of her pelvis with a sudden tightening in his throat, a fierce jolt of possessive need. And it was not the curve of her breasts or the length of her thighs or the sweet secret cradle of her hips that he found so intensely, irresistibly sexy, but the sight of her—her hair pulled back in a little ponytail, the shaggy ends making her look girlish and vulnerable, her face streaked with sweat, her muscles straining as she worked by his side. Just Lanie. That was all.

His voice sounded a little hoarse when he spoke. "Here. Wait a minute." He moved forward to lend his strength to hers, and together they pulled the branch free.

They stood close for a minute, breathing hard, sharing the satisfaction of accomplishment. Close enough to touch. Close enough to feel from each other how badly they needed to touch, to see it in each other's eyes. For a moment, standing in the steamy jungle sun with the drone of the insects in the background there was hesitation. Anything could have happened. But then Lanie smiled, a little uncertainly, and turned back to work. After a moment Chris did the same.

"You've raised two families," he observed after a time, his tone as casual as possible. "First your brother and sister, and now your sister's children. When's it going to be Lanie's turn? Don't you want children of your own, or are you tired of motherhood already?"

It was important, Lanie had noticed, to speak of possibilities, to talk about the things they had left behind as though their toil through the jungle were a mere stroll in the park after which they would pick up their lives where they had left off. She did not believe it of course, and neither did he, and when she talked about Cassie and Steve and the kids it was just a story.

They had become the fairy tale; only the here and now with Chris was real.

She laughed a little. "No, I'm not tired of it. I'm going to keep doing it till I get it right. What about you? You ever think about a family?"

"Oh, sure. Got to carry on the dynasty, and all that." He hesitated, and Lanie thought it was because he was having difficulty clearing a tangle of vines that had formed a web between two trees. She came forward to help, and his voice was a little subdued as he added, "I've been thinking about a lot of things more seriously lately." A husky, even fierce note came into his voice as he added, "I want a dozen. At least."

"Children?"

He glanced at her and the lightness in his tone seemed a little forced. "Of course, I might have a little trouble finding a woman who shares my enthusiasm, so maybe I'd better set my sights a little lower."

Ask me, Lanie thought.

After almost an hour of battling the deadfall Chris took off his shirt, and Lanie was distracted by the play of muscles in his back. She imagined the slippery, heated feel of his skin beneath her fingers.

Lanie remembered how easily, how casually they had become lovers, two strangers playing a game, acting out a harmless fantasy. But they weren't strangers anymore, and the wanting, the need, the *hunger* she felt for him had grown far more than sexual. Making love with him would only be a hollow imitation, a shallow expression of what she felt for him.

And so when the fever seized her and she looked at him it was with a fierce possessive pride, a throb of certainty that was primal and savage. *This is my man. Mine.* It had very little to do with the woman who had once lain with him in the soft light of a moon-drenched sea, or in fact with the man that woman had taken as her lover. He had been skilled and she had been eager; they had shared affection and humor and, perhaps, in their best moments, a wish that it could last longer, that it could be real. But those days were far behind them, as were the people they once had been. Nothing came easily anymore—especially not sex.

When Lanie shook herself out of her reverie, Chris was talking about his early childhood on Cape Cod, when the company headquarters was in New York, and about his brother, Anthony. "We were never very close," he was saying. He paused for a moment to wipe the perspiration from his eyes, then moved back to work.

"He was always a wimpy kind of kid, didn't like sports, almost drowned the first time my father tried to teach him to swim, and all those allergies..." He loosened the branch he had been wrestling with and tossed it aside, then tackled the large one it had supported. "He was never really good at anything, you know? I put him in charge of the L.A. office because I felt sorry for him, and because that's the kind of things brothers do, but west coast operations has gone steadily downhill since he took over. I probably should have fired him a long time ago." He straightened up, drawing a couple of deep breaths, squinting against the slanting rays of the sun. "I always counted on seeing him, again."

"To fire him?"

"No." He bent again to the stubborn branch, but paused for a moment to look at her. "Just to see him."

Lanie swallowed hard, fighting off a shiver of premonitory dread. "If you can move some of that rubble from the top, I think there'll be room enough for me to get in there and help."

After a moment he nodded, and did as she suggested. Together they moved the big branch, stepping back quickly from the avalanche of debris it sent tumbling.

Chris wiped his face with his forearm, breathing hard, as he surveyed the diminished deadfall. "That just might do it," he decided. He glanced at her. "You okay?"

Lanie, still gulping for breath after the exercise, nodded. He smiled and touched her shoulder, sliding his hand down her arm in a brief affectionate caress. "You're not a bad crew, you know that? Sit down and rest for a minute while I see if that thing will take my weight."

Her skin was still tingling from his touch, her chest aching from his smile. And as he started to move away she said, "No. We'll go together."

"Lanie..."

"We go together," she repeated firmly. "If you start to fall I'll be too far away to help you if I'm back here on the ground." She picked up the picnic bag and his shirt and handed them to him, her jaw set stubbornly, her eyes steady with the challenge. "Let's go."

Chris hesitated, clearly unhappy with the situation, but lacking an effective argument. He pulled on a shirt and draped the bag over his head. "Hold my hand," he instructed her. "And put your feet exactly where I put mine."

They started over the deadfall.

It was a nerve-wracking, painstaking climb. Debris shifted with every step, branches cracked, small creatures slithered away. Their hands were locked around each other's wrists but perspiration made their grasps tenuous. The tension of concentration was so thick it practically hummed in the air.

At last Lanie said, somewhat tightly, "Tell me about your house."

"It's a condo." Chris took a step forward, tested his weight on a branch and gave Lanie's wrist a gentle tug. "On the waterfront. Great view." The branch cracked as Lanie stepped on it and they both held their breaths, but it did not break. He hesitated before putting his foot forward again. "Funny, I don't really remember much else about it."

Lanie tried to imagine what it would be like to live in a place she couldn't even remember. But like so many other times that she tried to picture herself in Chris's world she drew a blank. And that blankness, like all the other times, left her feeling chilled and empty.

They reached the top of the deadfall and balanced there, looking down. The jump would only be about six feet, but it was littered with the pointed ends of sharp branches, hidden holes and tough vines, rotted limbs overgrown with foliage that could hide a nest of snakes. They looked at each other, and Chris gave her a smile for courage. "Your turn," he said. "Tell me about your house."

They started down.

He held her wrist tightly, balancing her as he picked his way cautiously down. She told him about the little house she shared with her sister and Chris tried to imagine what she described: suburbia, mowing the lawn, painting the eaves, shoveling the driveway. But the picture she painted was so far beyond anything in his experience. He wanted to learn about her life, but all Chris ever learned was that there was no common meeting ground for them...except, perhaps, the ground they were on now.

He released her hand and jumped the last few feet, then turned and grasped her waist, swinging her down beside him. She released a long breath of relief against his neck and said, "I don't mind telling you, that was pretty scary."

He held her close to him for just a second longer, feeling the softness of her breasts against his chest, the tautness of her waist, the heat of her skin. Every time he touched her it was harder to let her go.

Then he released her, and managed a grin. "Was it? I didn't notice."

She smiled at him, and they shared another one of those tentative, subtly charged moments in which anything was possible...and nothing was.

He turned away, searching for another sturdy limb to use as a walking stick. He found one and began to break the path ahead. "So," he invited easily, without looking back, "you were saying..."

DAY SIX.

The day was swollen with heat, and so thick that even the perpetual drone and chirp of the insects was muted. Chris and Lanie didn't walk so much as they swam, weighted down by their own sweat and the density of the day.

The picnic bag contained a few pieces of fruit and two bottles filled with water from a trickling spring they'd found the day before. It had taken almost two hours to fill them from the meager source that had dampened a fern-growing rock, and Chris didn't know when they would be even that lucky again, so the water was hoarded carefully.

The bag may have been lighter now but it felt as though it was filled with sand. With every step the contents jostled and bruised his hipbone. He had cut the sleeves out of his T-shirt to use as socks beneath the battered canvas deck shoes; they provided some protection but not much. Another three inches had been torn from the leg of his pants to use as bandages for the blisters on his feet and Lanie's. The pants themselves were torn and filthy, long since beyond recognition as ever having been white. Sometimes he tried to picture the expression on Madison's face if she could see him now, looking like a jungle commando from a low-budget action adventure film, and it made him smile. But he was having a harder and harder time picturing Madison's face at all.

It had been a long time since Chris had thought in terms of destination. The beach was no longer a reasonable goal, and rescue, possible contact with the outside world were concepts that barely existed even in the furthermost reaches of his mind. Today he would look for food. Tomorrow he would find more water.

Perhaps the day after that he would start building a shelter, a place to rest during the heat of the day, a refuge from the elements at night.

Meanwhile he told Lanie stories and fought the urge to begin each and every one of them with the preamble, "Long, long ago in a land far away..." Because that was exactly what the details of his life seemed like to him now.

"So anyway, that's when my dad decided to move the operation to Miami, which was long overdue if you ask me." He had been talking most of the morning, and his voice was starting to show the strain. "My mother lives in Palm Beach now, working hard at being a social snob and a charity queen."

"She sounds adorable."

"Actually, she is. Very few people can appreciate her. But I think you would."

"Chris, we're going to have to stop. It's too hot—"

She had been holding his hand over the rougher part of the terrain, steadying her steps with his sinewy strength. Now she stopped so suddenly that their hands, slippery with sweat, broke apart, and when Chris turned back to her she held up her fingers to still his alarm.

"Wait," she said softly. "Listen!"

She stood still and alert, her head cocked to listen and it came again, a distinctive *plop* on the leaves overhead, and another, and then a drop of water splashed on her arm.

"Rain," she whispered. She stared at the splash of wetness on her arm until it was joined by another, and another, and she cried, "Rain!"

She laughed out loud and stretched out her arms as the rain fell faster and faster, tilting her face up to taste the drops, exposing every available inch of skin to the fresh, cooling wetness. Chris was grinning, too, looking up through the trees at the darkening sky. Raindrops glistened on his beard and his hair. A surge of joy seized Lanie that carried with it a touch of madness, and she pushed past him to where the tree covering was not quite so thick, holding up her hands to catch the drops. By that time the shower was a deluge, pounding against the foliage and soaking her to the skin.

Lanie dropped to the ground and began searching through her purse.

"What are you doing?" Chris had to shout against the roar of the rain, and there was laughter and delight in his voice. He stood a few steps away from her, his hair slick and heavy with water, his clothes molded to his body, eyes narrowed against the rain that ran down his face and clumped his lashes together.

Lanie held up a travel-sized bottle of shampoo triumphantly. "Washing my underwear!" she cried, and stood up, peeling the tank top over her head. "Washing everything!"

Raindrops pelted her breasts with the stimulating force of a shower spray, cool against her hot and sticky skin, teasing her nipples to hardness, sluicing down her belly and her back. She unsnapped her culottes and pushed them and her panties down over her hips with a total lack of self-consciousness. She kicked them aside as she tilted her head back and let the rain spill over her body.

She was beautiful in her nakedness, slim and lithe and perfect, but it was not simply her beauty that went through Chris like a knife, that filled his loins to bursting, that paralyzed him with the need to freeze this moment, to hold it fresh and alive in his mind forever. It was Lanie, all of her. And whatever the future might hold, this moment would belong to them forever.

She spread her articles of clothing over the branches of a tree, then poured another measure of shampoo into her palms, working it into her hair, smoothing it over her face and throat. Chris stripped off his clothes and, naked and strong in his arousal, walked over to her.

Her eyes were dark and rich with light, blinking against the drops of rain that splattered over her face. He took the shampoo bottle from her and poured some of the liquid into his hand. She smiled at him, smoothing her soapy hands over his shoulders and down his arms, across his chest, sending stabs of pleasure through him with the firm drawing pressure of her fingers on the strength of his sex. He tasted the rain on her lips and the quickening of her breath. He massaged her shoulders, her back, her buttocks, her legs, rain sluicing away the soap between their bodies. He traced the shape of her nipples with slippery fingers, drawing out the hardened tips, watching with burgeoning delight as her eyes widened with pleasure and the smile on her lips faded into passion.

Lanie's head dropped back, arching her throat to the pressure of his lips, and she thrust her fingers into his heavy, wet hair. His beard was soft against her neck, not scratchy like she had thought, and his body was strong and hard, cool and slick with rain yet steamy with the heat that grew between them.

He slipped his hand between their bodies, pressing the tight concavity of her belly, tangling his fingers in the dark thatch of hair, and thrusting lower, parting her thighs. Her gasp of pleasure was lost in his mouth as he pushed his fingers inside her. The heat swelled and blossomed between them as the roar of rain poured down upon them, a madness of unleashed need that went deeper than desire, was more powerful than passion. Her arms tightened around his neck and her leg encircled one of his, knee pressing against his hip while her foot caressed his thigh. He tore his mouth from hers and her teeth sank into his neck as he moved his hands beneath her, lifting her effortlessly until her legs were locked around his waist and he plunged inside her.

Her cry was muffled by the roar of the rain and then by his mouth. She began to convulse around him even as he spilled himself inside her and they clung to each other, helpless against the power that exploded between them.

It was a release they both desperately needed, swift and intense, and as the spasms passed they sank together to the ground, drained by the physical power of it even though the tip of their passion was barely sated.

Chris arched his back as he withdrew from her, kissing her breasts and her stomach, holding her knees on either side of him, kissing the inside of her thighs. Her eyes were closed against the patter of rain, her face flushed, her breath quick and light. He stretched over her, taking the rain on his back, and already he was hard again. Her fingers closed on his arms as he sank into her, slowly, carefully at first because he was afraid he had hurt her before, but then as her face softened with rapture, as her eyes opened to meet his and her hips shifted to accommodate him he pushed deeper, and deeper still until he was buried in her, consumed by her.

She wrapped her arms around him, arching toward him, and the raindrops on her cheeks looked like tears. "Chris..."

"I know," he whispered, and he slipped his arms around her, drawing her against his chest, not moving inside her, just holding her. They stayed like that, fused together in silent communion and a depth of longing richer than mere physical expression could satisfy, for a long time.

The pounding of the rain lessened, fading at last to a steady sprinkle that caressed Chris's back, gathered on the ends of his hair and trickled down his shoulders, across his chest, and onto Lanie's breasts as he lifted himself above her. Taking his weight on his elbows he smoothed the wetness from her face with both hands.

"I can't promise you tomorrow," he said huskily. "I can't promise you anything. I don't even know what's real anymore. But I love you."

"I know." She lifted her hands to his face, her eyes brimming with adoration and tenderness and all the helpless longing that swelled inside her soul. "I know."

She pulled him down to her again as their bodies sought to express what words could not. And for that time, that fragile, wondrous, world-changing hour, forever belonged to them.

DAY EIGHT.

They had given up trying not to talk about food. Lanie called it creative visualization; to Chris it was the last grim defense against hopelessness, a reason to keep moving. Maybe there wasn't a seven-course meal waiting at the end of the journey but as long as they could convince themselves there might be they were able to continue to put one foot in front of the other.

"A steak," he said. "Rib eye, about the size of my hand, two inches thick and so rare it's practically still kicking."

She groaned. "Please. If you have to fantasize, couldn't it be about something that doesn't make me gag?"

"Yeah, well, finger sandwiches and fruit salad might be okay for you but we pirates need the taste of blood every now and then."

"Maybe you could kill me a quiche when you get the chance."

He grinned over his shoulder at her. The going seemed a little easier today; the ground was sandier and the foliage not so thick. Still, he was exhausted and a little light-headed, breathing hard after only a couple of hours' walk. Neither of them had had anything to eat since yesterday morning, and he knew they would not be able to walk much farther today.

He waited for her to catch up, holding aside a palm branch for her, then forged ahead. "Have you noticed?" he said. "The air smells a little different today. Cooler, maybe."

"Ice cream," she said. "Chocolate chip. A gallon of it to start, with caramel sauce on the side."

Chris's foot crunched something hard and cylindrical. He stopped short, so abruptly that Lanie almost bumped into him.

"Chris?"

He didn't answer. He didn't move.

"Chris, what's wrong?" Alarm threaded through her voice. "Are you okay?"

He was afraid to look. His heart was pounding in his ears and fresh beads of sweat broke out on his forehead. He moved his foot. Slowly, he bent down and picked the object up.

A crushed soft drink can.

He stared at it, swallowing hard, and had to take several slow deep breaths before he could even turn and show it to Lanie.

She took the can in her hands as though it were a treasured religious relic or a precious museum artifact. Tears flooded her eyes. She went into his arms wordlessly.

They had made it. They were going home.

Chapter Eleven

Half an hour later they came upon a picnic bench; by that time they could hear the cry of a gull and hear the ocean breeze rustling the treetops. Ten minutes after that Chris found the pavilion, and they followed the truck trail to the warehouses and the prefab building that was the caretaker's cottage.

Chris tried the door in a perfunctory manner, then walked around to the side window. "Give me your purse."

She did so at once. "What are you going to—"

He held the purse by its straps, testing its weight, then drew back and swung it hard at the window. The glass fell inward with a tinkling sound.

"Be careful," Lanie said anxiously as he reached through the broken pane to unlock the window.

He turned his head to look at her, and it struck them both at once with absurd hilarity: that after all they had been through, she should worry about him cutting his finger on a sliver of glass while trying to break into the place they had almost died trying to reach. He burst into laughter, and so did she, and they were still laughing when he unlocked the front door from the inside and swept her into his arms, carrying her over the threshold like a bride.

"There's a shower, Lanie!" he declared, whirling her around. "And a bed with sheets, and—"

He deposited her unceremoniously in the middle of the floor, where she staggered backward, gasping with laughter and delight, and he flung open the refrigerator door. "Damn! They cleaned out the refrigerator! Except..." He pulled out a six-pack of beer, tore two cans from the plastic holders and tossed one to her, ripping the pull tab of the other.

"Beer," she said wonderingly, turning the cold aluminum can over in her hand. It felt strangely alien yet wonderfully familiar. She'd never expected to hold a can of beer in her hand again.

Chris took a long drink, sagging back against the refrigerator. "Yes," he said, savoring the taste, and the word, on his tongue. "Oh, yes."

He pushed away from the refrigerator. "There's got to be a set of keys to the warehouses around here somewhere. Let's find them while I'm still sober enough to remember what I'm looking for."

Lanie opened the can and inhaled the aroma as though it were the bouquet of an aged wine. They had had beer, she and Chris, at twilight on the *Serendipity*. Weeks ago? Days? Or a few hours?

The first sip went straight to her head, actually making her laugh with silly surprise. She raised the can in a salute to Chris, opening her mouth for some profound remark, but then stopped. He stood in the middle of the room, staring at something, and he wasn't smiling anymore. Lanie followed his gaze, and abruptly her head cleared. She was as sober as she had ever been in her life.

They should have seen it the moment they walked in. It sat against one wall on a stand of its own, sleek and gray and businesslike.

The radio.

Salvation, civilization, home. The thing they had fought their way through the jungle for, the promise of rescue, justice for those who had stranded them here, safety. The final indisputable evidence that they had made it, the ordeal was over; it all had been worth it because now they were safe.

Chris walked over to it slowly. A flick of the switch and the helicopter blades would start to spin, coast guard sirens would whine, planes would stand ready on runways. A flick of the switch stood between him and Armani suits, black-windowed limousines, satellite relays and members of the board. He put his hand on the on/off lever. And he couldn't make himself move it.

Lanie stood beside him. Their eyes met and there were no secrets there. Outside this small island there were no promises, no guarantees; they had both endured too much and learned too much over the past week to deceive themselves about that. Outside the tight and insular world they had forged between them their separate lives awaited, and neither of them knew whether what they had found together would survive in the real jungle of the everyday world. For eight days they had battled thirst and starvation and oppressive heat and failing hope, they had braved the dangers of an alien, primitive environment and they had faced their own mortality; they had survived for this moment. Chris could not turn the switch. Lanie could not ask him to.

Chris couldn't take his eyes from hers. "I should register a distress call." *Don't make me. Not yet.*

Lanie's voice was a little hoarse. "Are we in distress?" *Don't let it be over. Not yet.*

He let his hand fall away from the switch. "I never felt less in distress in my life."

She stepped into his arms and they held each other tightly, fiercely, and for a long time. Then he grasped her shoulders and looked down at her, his eyes glowing with the soft fire of sun on water. "Now," he said, "let's eat."

There were no steaks in the big freezers, neither was there any ice cream. But they feasted on hamburgers and hot dogs and potato chips and cookies. They drank too much beer, they stood under a hot shower until it ran cold, they made love on clean white sheets. And for one more night they kept the world at bay.

IN LANIE'S DREAM she was running through the jungle, looking frantically for Chris, pursued by a giant flying reptile. Streams of bilious green flowed on either side of her, flashed before her eyes in the form of sharp-edged leaves that sprang up to block her way, slicing at her hands and face. She tried to scream for Chris but couldn't make a sound; the thing that was chasing her grew closer, the beating of its leathery wings pounding the air, growing closer and closer, and she knew if she could only find Chris she would be safe but he wasn't there. . . .

She awoke with a start, filmed with perspiration, terrified and disoriented but aware of two things: Chris was not there, and the beating of the leathery wings was growing louder. Sunlight streamed over a rumpled bed and bounced off the white walls of an unfamiliar room and for a single heart-stopping moment Lanie was seized by a terrible certainty that it all had been a dream, she had never flown to Miami or gotten on the wrong boat or been stranded on an uninhabited island or fallen in love with a fairy tale. None of it had really happened, and she was now waking in some hotel room in Cedar Rapids, Iowa that she had never left.

And then she saw him, a fuzzy, sun-blurred silhouette standing before the window, and her heart started beating again. But what was that *sound?*

She sat up. "Chris?"

He turned. "It's a helicopter."

A heaviness grew in her chest and seemed to freeze there. So soon! She hadn't counted on its being so soon. There was so much she wanted to tell him. "Did you . . . ?"

He shook his head, frowning. "You didn't?"

"I wouldn't know how!"

He turned back toward the window. "It sounds like it's landing."

"I—"

He looked at her, and suddenly all those things she wanted to say choked in her throat. All she could manage was, "We'd better get dressed."

They had barely stepped out of the cottage door when a woman, tall, rail-thin and wearing jungle fatigues—complete with combat boots—strode into view. Her hair was iron-gray and shorter than Chris's, her voice almost as deep. She gave Chris a quick but thorough inspection with her eyes, ending with a curt nod. "Glad to see you in good health, sir." She transferred her gaze to Lanie. "Miss Robinson, I presume."

"You have to be Madison," Lanie said.

"I do indeed. Pleased to make your acquaintance."

Incredibly the other woman extended her hand and Lanie was almost too dazed to take it. Madison took her hand in a firm businesslike grip and shook it once, hard.

Chris said, "For God's sake, Madison, how did you—"

"A rather long story, sir, which I'd prefer to tell you in the chopper if you don't mind. There's a matter of some urgency that requires your attention, and we'll be flying directly to the airport."

Chris looked at Lanie. They both felt everything start to spin out of control and neither knew how to stop it. Yesterday, eternity had been captured in the space between one breath and the next. Today... time had run out.

"I'll get my purse," Lanie said.

And just like that, it was over.

After they reached the chopper, everything was a blur for Lanie. There were two seats behind the pilot and Madison sat in the copilot's seat. They had to put on earphones to block out the rotary noise and to hear what she was saying. To Lanie, the disembodied voice coming through the earphones made the entire experience seem that much less real.

"It was your crew, sir—an apparent attack of conscience. We received an anonymous tip about your situation late yesterday, but it wasn't hard to track them down. The *Serendipity* is fine, by the way, docked in Nassau. It seems they were worried about the young lady, sir. Apparently she wasn't part of the bargain and, well, they liked her. I came as soon as it was light enough to fly."

Chris's eyes met Lanie's and held them. Then a small frown shadowed his features. "But I don't get it. What bargain? What the hell was this all about?"

"The board meeting, sir. It seems there's been dirty work afoot, something in the nature of a hostile take-over—"

Chris jerked his eyes away from Lanie and to the back of the speaker's head. *"What?"*

"Without your vote it would have been a simple matter. However, we just have time to make Los Angeles before the meeting. I took the liberty of having the jet fueled and standing by."

Lanie took off her earphones. The words were already becoming garbled in her mind, a strange kind of culture shock, and none of it concerned her at all.

THE HELICOPTER LANDED in part of the airport Lanie had never suspected existed before, much less expected to see. Chris was deep in frantic conversation with Madison as they disembarked, bending low to avoid the wind from the blades, and Lanie had to run to keep up. When they were able to straighten up Lanie saw they were heading for a row of private planes parked on the tarmac. She knew she didn't belong there.

She touched Chris's arm. "Chris, I—"

He turned to her, and he too seemed to realize for the first time where they were and what was about to happen. In his beard and torn T-shirt and long thick hair he was for one beautifully perfect, heart-wrenching moment the man she knew, the man who belonged to this place. From the primitive jungle to one of the world's busiest airports in the blink of an eye—it was easy to be confused.

He held her arms, searched her face, the depths of his struggle apparent in his eyes. "Lanie, this is too much. It's happening too fast. We can't say goodbye like this."

But they both had known, surely they had known, that they must say goodbye sometime.

"Come with me—"

She shook her head. "I've got my ticket." She patted her battered purse, and even managed a smile. "And places to go."

"I can't let you go like this."

Madison stood a few feet away, her back politely to him but her impatience evident. Chris cast a quick, frustrated glance in her direction. "Look, I have to take care of this. I don't know how long it will take. If you won't come with me—"

"You know I can't."

Sadness and resignation filled his eyes, along with a slow and final understanding. "Right," he said quietly. "You have a life."

Lanie touched his face, the rough texture of his beard, the smooth curve of the bone beneath his eye. "I love you," she said, and that was the hardest part. Loving him and letting go. Her voice tightened and almost broke, but she strengthened it determinedly. "I have from the beginning."

He smiled, and kissed her forehead. "I know."

A hot breeze wafted over them, bringing with it the scent of jet fuel and the roar of engines. Chris slowly lowered his eyes and released her arms. He turned and walked away.

"Hey."

He turned back and she smiled.

"It was one hell of an adventure," she said.

For a moment she thought he would come to her, sweep her into his arms and carry her away, and if he had she would have gone with him, she wouldn't have questioned, she wouldn't have protested. But then Madison touched his arm and said something to him in an urgent undertone.

The look he gave Lanie just before he hurried toward the waiting plane broke her heart.

Lanie turned in the opposite direction, in search of her own way home.

Chapter Twelve

All the way across the country Chris kept remembering what Lanie had said: *There are certain things in this world you can have, and certain things you can't. The trick is to know the difference.* Why did Lanie have to be the only thing in the world he wanted now—and the one thing he couldn't have?

With her typical efficiency, Madison had provided Chris with a change of clothes. As he washed and changed in the plane's small lavatory he felt as though he were putting on a costume—soft cotton underwear, blindingly white shirt, silk tie, silk socks, custom-fitted suit—just another actor stepping into another role. Would it be that easy to leave behind the man he had become, or almost become, in the past week? He did not shave, and tied back his hair at the nape with a rubber band. The man who strode into the boardroom of the Los Angeles office twelve minutes after the meeting was scheduled to start would have elicited more than a few stares under the best of circumstances, but it was not his hair or his beard or his lean, taut face that froze everyone at the table when he entered the room. They looked at him half in shock, half in awed fear, as though some primitive creature had suddenly invaded the sanctum of their civilized world and that, Chris registered with one small part of his mind, answered one question. It would not be so easy to leave behind the man he had become.

Anthony was saying, "... but I will be voting his shares, as you'll see on page three of..."

And when he noticed the sudden stillness at the table and looked up, the color drained from his face with an abruptness that was startling to watch.

Chris smiled. "What's the matter, Anthony?" he demanded quietly. "You look like you've seen a ghost."

Anthony's throat worked, but he said nothing.

Chris moved toward the head of the table smoothly. "It won't be necessary for you to exercise my proxy, as I'm perfectly capable of voting my own shares. But I do thank you for the offer and I wonder, gentlemen—and ladies—if we might have a short adjournment while I familiarize myself with the agenda."

Chris never took his eyes from Anthony and his brother seemed incapable of moving or speaking or diverting his glance. There was the shuffling of movement and murmur of voices as the other board members left. Someone touched Chris's shoulder and said, "I thought there was something wrong about this from the first." And another, "Glad you were able to make it, Chris." Then they were alone.

"You son of a bitch."

It was odd. Until he spoke those words Chris's fury at his betrayal had been hot and blinding and all consuming. Now suddenly he realized it wasn't the fact that his own brother had tried to steal his birthright and his company, but that because of Anthony he had lost Lanie. She was gone, and until that moment he had not fully realized that. When he did, the anger drained away and left in its place only hurt and confusion.

"Why?" he demanded quietly. "What did I ever do to you?"

Anthony looked away.

"I could have died," Chris said slowly. "Was it that important to you, do you hate me so much, that you would leave me there to die?"

Anthony burst out with sudden shocking bitterness, "You wouldn't have died. You're too perfect to die!"

Anthony pushed up from the chair and went over to the window, standing with his back to Chris. The silence went on for a long time. Then Chris said quietly, "Talk to me, Anthony. What's this all about?"

Anthony replied without turning. "Well, I got your attention anyway. That's the first time you've ever said that to me."

"What the hell are you talking about, Anthony?"

His brother turned on him. "I'm talking about me, about us, about this company! About the fact that you haven't bothered to read a single memo I've sent you in five years and as a result you're forced to close down west coast operations. About the fact that I could have saved us over half a million a year in operation expenses on Player's Cay and almost four million when we relaunched the *Rendezvous!* And I'll tell you something else—if you hadn't showed up today, if you'd given me a chance to present my case, the rest of the board would've voted with me, not because I had your proxy but because I was *right.*"

Chris stared at him. "What case? Will you for God's sake get to the point?"

"The point is that you're not fit to run this company, Chris," Anthony said flatly. "You're too busy playing heir apparent to even know what's going on, or care. If we leave control in your hands Holland-Alaska will be bankrupt in three years and I've got the figures to prove it."

Chris felt as though he'd been punched in the stomach. For a long time he could do nothing but stare at his brother and even when he spoke it was hard to summon up the indignation he should have felt. There was too much of him that recognized the truth. His voice was hoarse. "And you could do a better job, I suppose?"

Anthony swallowed hard and met Chris's eyes courageously. "Maybe not now," he admitted. "I have a lot to learn and you've never given me a chance to learn it. I would have employed a consultant to see us through the transition. But eventually—yes, I think I could have done a better job. You see..." and he made a small gesture with his wrist that for one brief moment took Chris back to their childhood in an oddly poignant way "...I like my work. It's all I have. And I guess that's the main difference between us."

The silence went on even longer this time, and Anthony didn't flinch from it. Then Chris pulled out a chair and sat down. He poured himself a cup of coffee from the silver pot in front of him.

"Sit down, Anthony," he said. "Let's talk."

MADISON FELL INTO STEP beside Chris as he emerged from the boardroom. "Will we fly back to Miami tonight, sir?"

"No." Chris's tone was decisive and precise. "Make sure my suite at the Hilton is available, and then get Fowler and Marshall out here—I want to see them first thing in the morning. Better put Ferguson on alert, too, and that guy in Sales—what the hell's his name?"

Madison had pulled a steno pad from somewhere and was taking notes, keeping up with his long stride effortlessly. "Metzenbaum, sir."

"Right. We'll probably need him out here by—" He paused, frowning at her. "What day is this, anyway?"

"Monday, sir."

With only a moment's hesitation he picked up the pace again.

"Then get him here by Thursday. Go get yourself some dinner and meet me back here at seven. We're about to undergo a major structural reorganization and I'll need you to document the first meetings."

Madison's pen paused over the page only for a fraction of a second. "Certainly, sir. May I ask exactly how major this reorganization is to be?"

Chris grinned. "Major. For one thing, I'll be delegating a lot more responsibility, and one of the recipients of that responsibility will be you. I hope you'll be willing to take over the management of the Miami office."

Not even a blink of the eye revealed Madison's surprise. "I'll do my best, sir. Thank you."

"For another thing..." Chris glanced down at her "...we're going into the boat-building business."

Madison looked at him, then nodded briefly. "I think your Grandpa Hannibal would approve."

Chris smiled. "I think so, too."

He resumed his brisk pace. "I'm on my way to Anthony's office. See if you can find me some dinner too, will you, and have it brought down. A steak would be good. Rare. All the trimmings."

"Right away, sir. And if you don't mind my saying so, sir—and I mean this in the best possible way..." Madison looked him over, thoroughly and assessively "...You've changed."

Chris smiled at her but it was a sad expression, and tired. He said simply, "I know."

His brother's office was lit only by the glow of a single lamp, and Chris did not enhance the illumination as he went straight to the bar and poured himself two fingers of Scotch. Out of habit he started to make himself at home behind the desk, then veered away with a wry shake of his head and chose the client's chair instead. It was more comfortable anyway, and he leaned back, swinging his feet up on the hassock, sipping his Scotch.

Anthony's office was not as visually appealing as his own, despite the spectacular view of downtown Los Angeles from the windows behind the desk. It was too dark, too utilitarian. The only spot of warmth in the room was the portrait on the opposite wall of the company's founder, Hannibal Vandermere.

He was a shrewd-looking cuss, Chris observed absently, sipping the whiskey. Dark red hair, narrow green eyes, and looking as stiff and impatient in his portrait finery as Chris felt in his suit and silk tie. Without thinking about it all, Chris began loosening that tie, kicking off his shoes.

He was doing the right thing, he was sure of it. There had never been anything wrong with him—or Anthony—except that neither one of them was doing what he was most qualified for. What he wanted to do, *needed* to do. There were some who would say Chris was taking a chance, dumping the entire operation in Anthony's lap while he took off a year to sail around the world, but for Anthony that was the only way he would ever have the freedom to make the company his own, and for Chris, taking chances was what life was all about. Hannibal would have understood, and approved. He was doing exactly the right thing.

Then why did he feel so empty?

Chris shrugged out of his jacket, unbuttoned the top two buttons of his shirt and tugged the rubber band out of his hair. He tucked it into his pocket and was surprised when his fingers touched something. Curious, he pulled out the contents of his pocket, which he had unthinkingly transferred from the other pants.

A broken comb. A soiled piece of string. An almost-empty tube of lip balm. A book of matches. Beef Man. Family Night Special—$4.95.

He turned the book over and over in his fingers, looking at it without really seeing it, thinking. And slowly a smile began to soften his tired features. Because there was just one more thing Grandpa Hannibal would have done.

He returned the matches to his pocket, and lifted his glass to the portrait in a broad salute. "Here's to possibilities."

Still smiling with the richness of triumph, he drank the contents down.

"I KNOW EXACTLY how long it takes to fix a closet door, Mr. Calvera," Lanie said into the phone. "I was in the construction business for over ten years. I also know that you've been promising to send someone up to do it for the past three days. So here's the deal. You have someone at my door, toolbox in hand, by..." she glanced at her watch "...noon today or I'll just have to tackle that closet door myself. And Mr. Calvera," she added sweetly just before she hung up, "*I* have a chain saw.

"That should do it." She replaced the receiver with a satisfied smirk and turned her attention to the whistling teapot behind her. Her teapot, her stove, her new apartment.

A month ago she never would have had the nerve to talk to her landlord like that. But she'd changed, as those who knew her never seemed to tire of pointing out—usually with dazed, confused expressions on their faces.

When she'd moved to the apartment in Cedar Rapids—a block away from the campus where she would be starting classes next month—her brother had been dumbfounded, her sister close to hysterical. But they would survive. And so would Lanie. She had several free-lance bookkeeping jobs lined up, enough to allow her to pay her rent and still attend college full-time. It wouldn't be easy, but she didn't mind at all.

It seemed to take Lanie forever to get over waiting for Chris—rushing to the phone every time it rang, eagerly searching through the mail for a letter or a card. He might have at least said goodbye. He might have let her know...

But "might haves" were foolish and futile. He had made her no promises and she had asked for none. He had given her the biggest adventure of her life, he had given her courage, confidence, memories enough for a lifetime; he had given her herself back. So it wasn't exactly happily ever after, but it was enough.

It would have to be.

The day was crisp and snow-locked, and bright light bounced off the floors and walls of the little apartment which was, at present, little more than a maze of unpacked boxes and unarranged furniture. Lanie had been unpacking all morning, and now she took her tea into the living room, sat down on a clear spot on the sofa, swung her legs up on a box and looked around in quiet satisfaction. Her apartment. Her quiet time.

Her life. Sometimes she couldn't believe it was really happening. Sometimes dreams really could come true.

Or almost.

There was a knock on the door and she glanced at her watch with a raised eyebrow and a satisfied nod. Four and a half minutes. "Now, *that's* more like it," she declared and put the teacup aside. She made her way as quickly as possible through the labyrinth of boxes and discarded packing material and at the last minute she remembered to call, "Who is it?"

"Prince Charming."

Her breath stopped, her feet stopped, the whole world stopped moving. She heard every individual beat of her heart but never knew when her hands moved, turning locks, lifting bolts, opening the door.

He was wearing a down jacket and jeans. His tan had faded somewhat and his beard was gone, but his eyes were still the color of sunlight on the sea. He was everything she remembered and nothing like what she remembered. He was the only thing she had dreamed of in all her life.

Her heart was roaring, thundering in her chest so loudly she could hardly hear her own words. She never expected to be able to breathe normally again.

"What took you so long?" she finally said.

At her words they moved into each other's arms and were crushed together. Fiercely his mouth covered hers, blinding her with the rush of heat and dizziness and exploding colors. His arms were like steel bands around her, pressing her to him until she seemed to melt into him, flowing like lava into his pores. Their kiss was greedy, starving lovers presented with a feast, breath-robbing, pulse-stripping, and it ended as abruptly as it had begun. They stepped away as though on a single thought, his hands hard on her arms, her fingers closing tightly on his.

His face was flushed, his eyes like coals as they moved over her. His voice was husky when he finally spoke. "A lot has happened."

"For me, too."

"None of it as important as what happened to me on that island."

"Me, too."

Again his mouth sought hers and Lanie thought if it were possible to die of happiness, she would have done so at that moment.

He lifted his face, his eyes brilliant and tender. "The University of Miami has a great astronomy program."

"I know. I was going to transfer there."

His hands cupped her face, fingers threading through her hair even as his smile went straight through her soul. "But in the meantime, there's supposed to be a lunar eclipse at the end of the month that's drawing astronomers from all over the world to the coast of Guatemala. I can offer you the best seat in the house—right on the deck of the *Serendipity.*"

Lanie's heart was pounding so hard she could barely hear herself think. All she could see was his face, his beautiful, brilliant, sea-roving eyes. Eyes that darkened a shade now, becoming tinged with anxiety.

"I'll show you the world, Lanie, if you'll show me the stars. So what do you say? Shall I take you away from all this?"

He actually looked as though he wasn't sure she would say yes. As though he was afraid she wouldn't. But Lanie couldn't stop smiling. She couldn't stop touching him, filling her eyes with him. "Happily ever after?"

Some of the anxiety faded from his eyes. "Or a reasonable facsimile thereof."

She brought her hand to his face, caressing the shape of his cheekbone. "You know," she said softly, "I really don't believe in fairy tales."

He smiled. "I know. But sometimes…" she felt the deep expansion of his chest with a long slow breath as he drew her into his arms again, holding her, sheltering her, adoring her "…love makes it real."

And so it did.

ABOUT THE AUTHOR
The versatile Rebecca Flanders is a familiar name to readers of
American Romance. Since 1983, when she supplied the introductory
sampler to the series, she has written over a score of American Romance
novels. In addition, she's the author of romantic suspense, mainstream
and historical romance novels. Rebecca makes her home in the
mountains of Georgia, along with her teenage daughter.

Books by Rebecca Flanders
HARLEQUIN AMERICAN ROMANCE
167—AFTER THE STORM
183—PAINTED SUNSETS
257—SEARCH THE HEAVENS
357—THE SENSATION
417—UNDER THE MISTLETOE

HARLEQUIN INTRIGUE
 8—SILVER THREADS
13—EASY ACCESS

HARLEQUIN SUPERROMANCE
180—THE GROWING SEASON

Don't miss any of our special offers. Write to us at the following address
for information on our newest releases.

Harlequin Reader Service
P.O. Box 1397, Buffalo, NY 14240
Canadian address: P.O. Box 603,
Fort Erie, Ont. L2A 5X3

RFB10

HARLEQUIN®

I N T R I G U E®

A SPAULDING AND DARIEN MYSTERY

Amateur sleuths Jenny Spaulding and Peter Darien have set the date for their wedding. But before they walk down the aisle, love must pass a final test. This time, they won't have to solve a murder, they'll have to prevent one—Jenny's. Don't miss the chilling conclusion to the SPAULDING AND DARIEN MYSTERY series in October. Watch for:

#197 WHEN SHE WAS BAD by Robin Francis

Look for the identifying series flash—A SPAULDING AND DARIEN MYSTERY—and join Jenny and Peter for danger and romance....

HARLEQUIN
AMERICAN ROMANCE®

American Romance's yearlong celebration continues.... Join your favorite authors as they celebrate love set against the special times each month throughout 1992.

Next month... Spooky things were expected in Salem, Massachusetts, on Halloween. But when a tall, dark and gorgeous man emerged from the mist, Holly Bennett thought that was going too far. Was he a real man... or a warlock? Find out in:

OCTOBER

S	M	T	W	T	F	S
				1	2	3
4					9	10
11	12		15	16	17
18	19			23	24
25	26	27	28	29	30	31

#457
UNDER HIS SPELL
by Linda Randall Wisdom

Read all the *Calendar of Romance* titles, coming to you one per month, all year, only in American Romance.